When Cadets Don and Jim Mercer and their friend Terry Mackson were ordered by Colonel Morrell of Woodcrest Military Academy to gather together all the school trophies, they were able to find all except one—the cup awarded to the Class of 1933. What had happened to the cup was a mystery the boys were determined to solve. And little by little Don and Jim uncovered a strange story and unraveled a mystery that had puzzled school authorities for years. The Mercer boys uphold the honor of Woodcrest against a conspiracy of silence and dishonor.

THE MERCER BOYS' MYSTERY CASE

CAPWELL WYCKOFF

WILDSIDE PRESS

Originally published in 1948.
Published by Wildside Press LLC.
wildsidpress.com

Chapter 1
The Glories of the Past

A group of pleasant-looking young men, neatly dressed in the spruce, gray uniforms of the cadet corps of Woodcrest Military Institute, stood at ease in one of the halls downstairs in Locke Hall. They were representatives from the various classes, ranging from the senior, or first class, to the third or sophomore class. As yet the two representatives from the fourth or freshman class had not arrived, and it was for these two cadets that the others were waiting.

"A special meeting, huh?" spoke up Cadet Don Mercer, one of the representatives from the third class. "Anybody got any idea what Colonel Morell has in mind?"

"I haven't," replied Senior Cadet Captain Bob Hudson. "I guess none of us have. Farley and I got a notice to report to the study room here for a special meeting, and that's all we know."

"Here comes the rest of the party," announced the second class representative, as the two fourth class men hurried up. "Now as soon as the colonel comes we can get down to business."

It was a fall day at the military academy, and Colonel Morrell, the headmaster, had sent word early in the day that he wished to meet the leaders of the various classes briefly after the last lesson period. The boys were waiting now, talking light-heartedly among themselves, for they were all friends of long standing, except for the two men from the fourth class, who were newcomers.

Don Mercer, the cadet who had spoken first, was now entering his second year at Woodcrest Military Institute. With his brother Jim and his friend Terry Mackson he had entered the academy the previous year. Jim, Terry and Don were old friends, and their first real adventures had taken place two summers ago, when they had gone for a summer cruise and had captured some marine bandits, details of which were related in the first volume of this series, *The Mercer Boys' Cruise in the Lassie*. In the second volume, *The Mercer Boys at Woodcrest*, they came to military school and helped to solve the mystery of old Clanhammer Hall and to rescue their beloved headmaster, Colonel Morrell. Then, on the previous summer the three chums had taken a trip to Lower California with a former history teacher, Professor Scott, where, after many thrilling adventures, they had uncovered the buried wreck of a Spanish treasure ship. All of this, told in The *Mercer Boys on a Treasure Hunt*, had contributed to make their lives adventurous and active, and they were now back in school to take up the duties and pleasures of a new fall term.

Don and Jim Mercer were both healthy-looking young boys in their late teens, curly-haired, and well-built. Their friend Terry was tall, bony and red-headed, chiefly noted for a cheerful disposition and a wide grin.

A short fat man came rapidly down the hall, a good-humored-looking man who was nearing old age but who was not allowing it to get the better of him. He was clad in the gray uniform of a cadet colonel, the sight of which brought the cadets to instant attention, although the colonel himself, and not the uniform, inspired their respect and sincerity. He was the idol of the school, for his sympathetic understanding had won all of the student body to him, and the young men of the cadet corps would have cheerfully gone to the end of the world for their headmaster. When the colonel approached the cadets, he gestured with his hand and said, "Rest."

"Well, young men, all here I see," remarked Colonel Morrell, as he opened the door of the study room. "Come right in and be seated. Make yourselves at home, as you generally do when you come here to study."

The colonel chuckled at his own joke. He knew that sometimes other things than study went on in the study rooms, but he had always known how to give his lively boys enough rope with which to have a good time, and at the same time just how far to go with them on the point of study. The result had been that the cadets had their fun and still kept up a good average of scholarship. They appreciated the headmaster's sally and entered the room. The colonel sat down in a large chair and they sat on the long window seats facing him.

"All of you are wondering what is in the wind, no doubt. I'll get to the point at once. All of you know that I have planned for some time to turn old Clanhammer Hall into an Alumni Hall. It has outgrown its usefulness as a school building, and yet its associations are so fine that we don't wish to tear the place down." He smiled at Don and continued. "Inasmuch as it once served the part of a prison for Mercer and me, we feel more sentiment for it than the rest of you do! But it is really a fine old place, and it will be the most fitting place in the whole school for our Alumni Hall.

"Now, in order to make that hall live in the memory of the men who will come back here on annual visits we must find all of the trophies that teams in the past have won. What made me think of it was this: I went into an old closet on the top floor of this hall yesterday and down in a corner I found a moth-eaten blue banner which the class of 1893 won in a football championship. I don't know if it is the right of a soldier to be sentimental, boys, but I couldn't help feeling as I saw the faded blue color and the small white letters that some fine young fellows had fought very hard in days gone by for that particular piece of cloth and what it represented, and that the bottom of an obscure closet was not the place for it. Later on, when I thought it all over I realized that we have been mighty careless here at Woodcrest in the matter of our trophies and the glories of the past."

"I have often wondered why we didn't have trophies around the school," smiled Cadet Douglas, Don's brother representative of the class.

"The whole trouble is that we have never had a regular committee to attend to that matter," the colonel explained. "Each class has won some kind of a trophy in years gone by and has cared for it just as they wanted to. Some few of them were hung up in the various study halls, some in the assembly room, and I'm afraid some of them have just been carelessly stowed away somewhere. I want all of you men, as representatives, to scour the halls from end to end and unearth as many of these emblems of victory as can be found. We'll check up against a list until we have all the trophies that Woodcrest ever received."

"Have you a list of all trophies, sir?" asked Hudson.

"No, but I know where we can get one. Ever since the founding of the school we have had our school magazine, the *Woodcrest Bombardment*, and surely each number will tell of the class winning any emblem and what that emblem was. Fortunately, you will find a complete set in the library, each monthly volume intact, and you will find the set of the greatest value in your quest. My suggestion is that the representative read through the school notes of each book and find out just what each class won and then make a list up, against which we will check the recovered cups, flags, banners or whatever we have."

"When we get them all it is your plan to place them in Clanhammer Hall, isn't it?" Don asked.

"Yes, that is my thought. Early this winter I want to open the old historic hall as the Alumni Hall. At that time I want to have the old graduates come back and see the banners and cups hanging on the walls, showing them that we of today appreciate their struggles, their spirit and their loyalty. Nothing keeps a school up like the spirit of loyalty and the remembrance of past deeds of courage and self-sacrifice. You boys can see how it is. If you won a silver cup for Woodcrest this year by hard, determined struggle you wouldn't want to come here to school ten years from now and find out that no one remembered the first thing about it or even so much as knew where the trophy was. I want all of those old students to come back here and see that the school remembers them and appreciates what they have done in the past to make the institution a place to be proud of."

"That's what I'd like to see," murmured Farley.

"Of course you would, we all would. Well, suppose we meet again on Friday afternoon at the same time and see what we have discovered? If you want to get into any closet or room that is locked up just let me know and I'll gladly give you the key. That will be all, boys."

After the colonel had left the room the cadets gathered to talk the situation over. They were all in favor of his plan and they felt confident that they would succeed in bringing to light all of the trophies of the past. Hudson suggested that they go directly to the assembly hall and make out a list of the things to be found in there. As there was still some time before drill they went in a body to the assembly room.

Douglas had a pad and pencil and noted down the trophies as they were called. In the general assembly room they found four banners, two silver cups, one silver football with a figure of a man running the ball mounted on it, and a wooden shield with two small cups on it, the result of a debating team victory. When these items had been written down they all bent over the pad in Douglas' hand.

"The red banner, the baseball trophy, is dated 1901," remarked Hendon, of the second class. "How far back do we have to go in the search?"

"How old is the school?" asked a fourth class man.

"The date on Clanhammer Hall is 1885," supplied Don.

"Then that is the date of the school," replied Hudson. "Clanhammer Hall is the original building, you know. I guess we'll find the initial number of the *Bombardment* is dated that year, too. So it looks as though we'd have to dig back a number of years."

"Yes, but the school didn't win a trophy every year," grinned Farley. "A good old school and all that, but it didn't win something every year."

"Perhaps not, but pretty nearly," came back Don. "Don't forget, there were baseball, football, basketball, track, debating and tennis teams, to say nothing of swimming teams. I guess we'll find there are quite a few trophies when we come to look for them."

The call for drill sounded and the cadets quickly separated to assemble with their several units. Don was now a lieutenant in the infantry, but Jim was far ahead of him in his particular section, the cavalry unit, the first man in the history of the school to attain that honor who was not in the second or first class. His steady attention to drill and his heroism in saving Cadet Vench on Hill 31 had placed him in that responsible position. Terry was, to use his own expression, "still coaxing the big ladies to speak out in meeting," by which he meant he was still serving in the artillery, around his beloved guns, whose workings fascinated him.

That evening in their room Don told Jim and Terry about the hunt for trophies. He had obtained some copies of the school magazine and together they pored over the early school notes. They found that there had been many trophies in days gone past.

"There must be some up in the storage room in the attic," Jim said.

"Yes, and I saw a battered cup in the locker of the senior study room," Terry said. "Looked like somebody heaved it at somebody else. After it has been repaired it will do very nicely to put on a shelf."

"I'm glad the colonel is going to fix up the old hall and set up the prizes," Don said. "I think every school should take pride in its past history."

In the days that followed the committee of young soldiers were very busy. During their spare hours between study, drill and classes, they scoured the school for trophies. The results were astonishing. From old closets, from lockers, from under window seats and from the storage room they brought cups, flags and banners. For some time they were baffled in their search for a big silver cup, but at last found it in the workshop of a former janitor, down in the cellar of the old school. Some of the flags came from the walls of dormitories, though most of them were in Locke Hall, the main hall of the school.

A careful list had been made from the back numbers of the school paper and at last all trophies but one had been found. By checking up they found that a silver cup, given to the class of 1933, was nowhere to be found. Had they gone to the colonel at once they would have saved themselves a lot of fruitless searching, but they did not and so after fairly turning the school upside down they had to admit failure.

"We'll have to admit we're licked on that cup," Hudson decided. "The meeting is to be this afternoon and if there is a corner in this school that we haven't peeked into I don't know where it is!"

The colonel met them that afternoon and was pleased with their good work. Hudson explained that fifteen flags and banners, three silver footballs, a number of trophy shields and ten cups had been found.

"These represent victories in every department of work, both athletic and scholastic," the cadet captain said. "The oldest banner is dated 1887 and is for a football championship. The last trophy is a silver cup dated 1947 and brings our list up to date. From now on we can keep a better record of our trophies and set them up in Clanhammer Hall as we get them."

"A total of fifty-five trophies," put in Douglas. "There are quite a number of shields with descriptive plates and small silver cups on them, the prizes of debating teams."

"Are they all in good order?" asked the colonel.

"Most of them are," replied Hudson. "Suppose we take a look at them soon and you may see for yourself. One or two of the cups have been bent and the banners are somewhat dirty and in some cases decidedly moth-eaten. But the lettering is all intact, even on the 1887 banner, and I'm sure we can exhibit them without fear of their falling apart."

"Then you have made a success of the job," began the

colonel, but Hudson stopped him.

"I'm afraid we haven't quite done that, sir," he said. "We cannot find the silver cup donated to the class of 1933 anywhere."

The colonel looked puzzled. "I don't remember that cup. What are the details?"

"According to the issue of the *Bombardment* of that time the cup was awarded by Melvin Gates to the school with the highest rate of individual scholarship, and Woodcrest won it, in fact, the son of the donor won the cup. Well, we cannot find that particular cup anywhere in the school." He paused as a look of recognition came over the colonel's face. "Do you remember it, sir?"

The colonel spoke slowly. "Yes, boys, from the details you have given, I do remember that cup. There is a story connected with it, a story that is by no means pleasant. I do not know where the cup is, but I'll tell you the story of its strange disappearance."

Chapter 2
The Class of 1933 Trophy

The cadets looked astonished and interested and waited in respectful silence as the headmaster thought for a moment to refresh his memory. Then, with the facts in his mind, he related the story.

"In 1933 there was some talk in the local newspapers about high scholarship among the preparatory and military schools and the idea was expressed that military schools gave so much thought and time to drill and military duties that it was impossible for them to produce a high rate of scholarship," the colonel began. "In the years which have passed since then we have shown here at Woodcrest that such was not the case, that we have turned out scholars as well as gentlemen and soldiers. I ignored it at the time, but one of the trustees, a man who is still trustee, Melvin Gates, became very much incensed over the article in the papers and took steps to challenge it. He conferred with me and I finally agreed to put up at least three cadets whom I thought to be the smartest in their classes, against any three from a preparatory school, and, after an elimination, to allow my brightest scholar to compete against another student from a preparatory school. This was done, and the boy who took the honors in this school was the Arthur Gates you mention, the son of the man who was to donate the cup. He beat the other two boys and won first place.

"A nearby preparatory school, Roxberry, then put forward its best scholar and the examination was held. It embraced every branch of the studies which every scholar is supposed to have had at this stage of preparatory school life, and to the joy of all Woodcrest students, Arthur Gates won it. The questions had been prepared by professors from Roxberry and instructors from this school and the two young men took the examination in a room entirely by themselves. The other student received a marking of ninety-five but Arthur Gates answered every question one hundred per cent. A truly remarkable thing when you think of it, and Woodcrest was mighty proud of him for it."

"Should think it would be!" murmured Douglas.

"The editor of the paper publicly agreed that he had been wrong in his estimation of military institutions and apologized. Roxberry graciously accepted defeat and we were just ready to award the cup to Arthur Gates when a very unfortunate thing happened. The cup disappeared!

"Just at this point I'll have to go back a little bit and tell you this fact: One of the cadets who was runner-up with Gates was a class captain named George Long. Long was a fine young man, with a splendid career before him, and he tried hard but was defeated by Gates. After his defeat he became entirely different from his usual self, turned quiet and moody and was seen to talk to Gates privately many times, at which times Gates seemed to say no, as though Long was making him some dishonorable proposition. Even when Gates won the scholarship for the school he was not happy and refused to congratulate him at all. We all put it down to jealousy and a bad school spirit, a thing which was hard to believe, for Long was always a gentleman, but that was his attitude. I suppose that he wanted to win that scholarship himself, as it was his last year in Woodcrest, and it was certain that some college, hearing of his success, would have awarded him a scholarship, which is just what they did to Gates, eventually.

"The senior Mr. Gates had turned the cup over to me and had asked me to present it to his son, as that would look better than it would for him to give it, but I wanted one of the student body to present it, as a mark of honor from the cadet corps. But if I did that Long would have to be the one to present it, as he was senior class captain and also captain of the infantry, and I didn't know how he would feel about it. So I asked him and he said that there was nothing wrong between Gates and himself and that he would gladly present the cup for the student body.

"I therefore turned the cup over to Cadet Captain Long on the night before the general assembly and he took it to his room. When the next day came all of the cadets assembled in the auditorium and there were guests of the school and representatives of the press in the room. But Captain Long was missing and I could not understand the circumstances. I began the exercises, hoping that he would come, but he did not and before long I was at the point where Arthur Gates was to have been presented with the cup.

"I immediately sent a cadet in search of Long, and the messenger found him in his room, frantically going through every

13

drawer and corner of the room. The cup had been stolen, he declared, sometime in the morning. I had to go up there myself, to find him half-distracted, turning everything inside out in his quest for the cup. It was not found, and I was forced to go back to the auditorium and explain the theft of the cup. The place was in an uproar and Melvin Gates was furious, but all we could do was to make young Gates stand up and honor him that way. There was simply no cup to be found and that was all there was to it.

"Afterward I had my hands full. The senior Gates wanted to arrest Long, believing him a thief, but although I didn't believe he was I couldn't understand what had happened to that cup. Gates himself, that is, Arthur Gates, had been in Long's room on the night before and had seen the cup on Long's dresser, and it had been there when Long went to bed and when he got up in the morning. It was after chapel that he had first noticed that it was gone, and he had hunted around for it without saying anything to anyone about it. Long had no roommate, so there was no suspicion there. I thought myself that he might have hidden the cup for a joke or even in a mean spirit, but he insisted that he had not done so.

"The newspapers rapped the cadet 'honor' severely and it was no easy task to remain patient under it all. Long did not resign or do anything foolish, he finished out the year, but under a distinct cloud. Arthur Gates took the loss of his cup calmly, continued to be Long's friend, and even made a fine speech about it all in assembly. The elder Gates was finally pacified and things died down, but search as we might, we never did find that cup.

"As I have said, Long finished out the year and graduated, but it was a hard job. You know it is the custom to clap when a senior goes up and receives his diploma, but when the cadet captain of the entire school went up there was only a silence, a brutal, condemning silence. I saw his face redden and harden as I gave him his diploma, and I pressed his hand hard, but he simply dropped mine and went back to his seat with his head held high. That looks as though he was not guilty and I'd like to think so, but the fact remains that everything is dead against Mr. Long. He had never been gracious about Gates' victory over him and never in the least bit generous in any way about it all, and no one could blame the cadets for feeling the way they did. I was severely scored by the papers for not dismissing him from school for neglect of duty if for no other cause, but I felt that would do no good and so I never went to such a limit. I will confess that I hoped and hoped that the cup would turn up some day and we'd find out it was just some prank or mistake, but it never did.

"We have had alumni meetings each year and Long never comes to any of them. I have purposely written to him more than once, although I don't know if that is quite wise, for the old graduates might turn the cold shoulder to him when they met him. But I wanted to see if he would come and face them in spite of it all, but he evidently does not want to do so. Gates doesn't come very often, in fact there are some fellows who have never returned to visit the old school once they left it, but that much is to be expected.

"Well, that's the story of the 1933 class trophy, boys. We have always called it that because both Gates and Long belonged to the senior class of 1933 and that class represented the whole school. It isn't a pretty story and I'm sorry that it ever happened. I guess we can count that trophy out and you may cross it off your list."

The colonel sighed as he concluded and the boys sat for a moment in silence. The honor and courage of his boys was a live issue with the colonel and it hurt him to think that any of them should not be worthy. Even though it had happened a number of years ago it was always a fresh hurt to him, and they suspected that he had always had an affection for Long.

"We're very sorry to hear that, Colonel Morrell," said Hudson, at last. "It certainly is mysterious, but all signals point to this Long. Very well, we'll cross that particular item off our list."

"Yes, the sooner we forget all that, the better," the colonel nodded. He got up briskly. "Suppose we go and take a look at the cups and banners now."

They filed out of the room and went down the hall to a smaller study room, where the school trophies had been placed. The colonel looked them all over with evident enjoyment, recalling incidents and stories about almost every one. He was well pleased with their work and expressed it.

"Now, the next step will be mine," he announced. "I'm going to have the old hall thoroughly cleaned and then some needed work done in it. After that we'll have our first big alumni meeting and you boys will be on duty that night, to share in the fun and listen to the talks. I thank you kindly, boys, for your good work. In the future we'll see to it that the school trophies are properly taken care of and that it will never be necessary for another committee to go around and pick up flags and cups."

"Well, that ends that," remarked Farley, as the cadets prepared to separate. "We'll have to add a few more to the collection this fall and winter."

"Yes," agreed Hudson. "Too bad about that 1933 cup."

"It certainly is," agreed Don, as the others nodded silently. "I'd like to get ahold of that cup and make it talk! No telling what it would say!"

"You are right there," laughed a third class man. "They say that dead men tell no tales, and I guess lost cups don't either!"

Chapter 3
A Mystery Uncovered

That night Don settled himself in his chair to study. Jim was across the room intent on history and Terry was visiting down the hall. The redheaded boy was unusually bright in his studies; he was going through Woodcrest on a scholarship which he had won, and he seemed to get along with very little study. So he was able to do a little visiting, while the others found that they must bury themselves in their books.

Don and Jim studied for some time and then Don felt that he had his lesson clearly in his mind. He glanced around the room and his eyes fell on some back numbers of the *Bombardment*, copies of which had helped in the search for the trophies. This copy at which he was looking was dated 1933, and Don idly looked through it, scanning the school and athletic notes of the period.

Presently a particular notice attracted his attention. It was an item in the school notes department, and read as follows: "John Mulford, our efficient and pleasant janitor for the past six years, left us quite unexpectedly this past week. We were unable to learn just why he left us. For the next few days the students will do well to thank their lucky stars that it is the spring and not the winter of the year."

Don passed the notice off lightly, wondering what it was that interested him in it at all. His eyes swept up the column and something else drew his attention. It was also a brief paragraph, but it started an idea in his mind.

"There has been a let-down to the social activities of the senior class since the regrettable affair of the Gates Scholarship Cup, but we hope that such a condition of affairs will soon mend."

His eyes narrowed slowly. Carefully he read the first note and then the second and tried to construct a picture in his mind. He placed the magazine back on the table and sat back in his chair, his eyes half closed. Jim looked up from his book.

"Better go to bed, instead of falling asleep there, kid," he advised.

"I'm not falling asleep, Jim," Don answered. "Listen here, I've got something on my mind, and I want your advice."

For some time he talked to Jim, who forgot his lessons in his interest. At last Jim slowly nodded his head.

"It sounds good to me. Are you going to tell the colonel in the morning?"

"Yes, the first chance that I get."

Just before his first class the next morning Don found Colonel Morrell in his study. The colonel motioned him to a seat.

"What is on your mind this morning, Don?" asked the headmaster.

"I was reading one of the back numbers of the *Bombardment* last night," Don replied. "And in it the distressing affair of the Gates Cup was mentioned. Right underneath it was mentioned the fact that a janitor by the name of John Mulford disappeared, or rather left the school for some unknown reason. Wasn't he suspected?"

"Yes, he was," returned the colonel, promptly. "In fact, I had him watched, but he didn't take a thing out with him."

"I see. Could it have been possible that he came back and got something later on?"

"Possible, but I don't think so. No, I'm pretty sure that he didn't have anything to do with it, in spite of his oddly abrupt leaving."

"My thought is that Mr. Long was never guilty, Colonel Morrell," Don went on. "I feel that something strange was connected with that whole case, and that your former captain suffered a grave injustice. I wonder if you'd allow me to do something?"

"What do you want to do, Mercer?"

"Do you know where this former janitor went?" Don asked.

"When he left here he went to live in Ashland, a small manufacturing town seventy miles east of here. I had to write to him once to send him some money due him, so I know that much. But whether or not he lives there now I don't know, of course."

"I see. Can you find that address and will you allow me to go to Ashland and talk to this man Mulford?"

For a brief instant the colonel studied Don's earnest face and then he nodded shortly. "Yes, I can do all of that," he said.

18

"You will want to go on a Saturday afternoon, won't you?"

"Yes, sir. You have faith in my idea, colonel?"

"Not as much faith in your idea as I have in you," returned the colonel. "I know what you are capable of. I too have never believed Long guilty, and I'd like to see him cleared."

"Thank you," said Don, as he left the room. "I'll go next Saturday, Colonel Morrell."

Nothing more was said on the subject until the following Saturday morning, at which time the colonel gave Don a slip of paper with the name of a street in Ashland on it. While the other cadets were out on the field waiting for a football game to begin Don left the school and boarded a train for Ashland.

"I don't know that this isn't a wild goose chase for fair," he reflected, as the swift train bore him across the country. "But I'm willing to make an attempt to find out what happened to that cup."

It was late in the afternoon when he reached the manufacturing city, and after some inquiries he located the street on which the former janitor had lived. Don finally found the house, a narrow affair of red brick, sandwiched in between high rows on either side. He rang the bell and at last it was answered by a tall, thin girl.

"Does Mr. Mulford live here?" Don asked, raising his hat. He was not dressed in his uniform, as that would have attracted too much attention, but was clad in a plain everyday dress suit.

"Yes, he does," was the gratifying answer. That was all the girl said, and she seemed to be waiting for something else.

"Can he come to the door?" Don went on, seeing that she did not intend to say anything more.

"No, he can't. He ain't walked for seven years," was the startling answer. "He's crippled!"

"Oh," exclaimed Don. "I'm very sorry to hear that. Then I suppose I can't see him?"

"Sure you can, if you'll come upstairs," the girl said. "On business, is it?"

"Yes," answered Don.

The girl led the way up a flight of dark stairs into a small room which was hot and in which a variety of cooking odors hung in the air. An old man was sitting in a wheel chair near a window, looking out into the gathering darkness of the street below. He had a pale face and white hair, and Don could see that his lower limbs were thin and gathered up.

19

"Somebody here to see you on business, pa," said the girl, and to Don's relief she quit the room at once.

Mulford looked curiously at Don, who was not certain what to do. He had not expected to find the former janitor a cripple and he wondered if he should question a man in this condition. Mulford spoke up in a voice that was full and strong.

"What did you wish to see me about, young man?" he asked. "Sit down, won't you?"

Don sat down facing the man. "I am from Woodcrest School, Mr. Mulford," he began. "I understand that you were once janitor there, and I came to see you about something that happened years ago. But perhaps I had better not say anything about it. I didn't expect—didn't——"

"You didn't expect to find me a cripple, eh?" finished Mulford, quietly. "I wasn't one when I left the school. So you are one of the cadets there? I'm glad to know you. I liked all of those boys when I was there. What can I do for you?"

"Well, it's rather a delicate subject," began Don. "Mr. Mulford, if you feel that I'm prying into any of your private affairs you just tell me to get out of here and I'll go. But first let me tell you a story. You remember George Long and Arthur Gates, don't you? They were students there when you left so unexpectedly."

Mulford's face was a study. He looked fixedly at Don and was silent for a moment. Then he said something that astonished the cadet.

"Yes, I knew them. I'm glad you came here, young man. I've had something on my mind for a number of years and I want to get it off. I haven't had the nerve to write to Colonel Morrell about it myself, but I have wanted to. You want to know about that silver cup, don't you?"

Don was staggered. He nodded.

"As soon as you mentioned the name of Gates and George Long I knew what you had in mind," the man said. "You want to know what I know about that cup. I'll tell you right now that I didn't take it myself, and if you had come to me some years ago I would have driven you out of the door. But this ailment of mine has tamed me down a whole lot and I've had nothing to do but think for several years. Do you people at the school think I took it?"

"Colonel Morrell doesn't," Don answered. He went on to

tell of the search for the trophies of the past and the story of the missing cup. "For years George Long has been suspected of having taken that cup," he went on. "He graduated under a cloud and has never come near the school since. What we are trying to find out, even at this late date, is whether he did take it or not."

"I thought something like that would happen," the former janitor said, closing his eyes. "I'm responsible for it, too. No, young man, George Long didn't take that cup. Arthur Gates stole that cup himself, on the morning it was to have been presented to him!"

"What! He stole his own cup!" cried Don, open-mouthed.

"Yes, and I saw him do it. He came out of Long's room with it in his hands, trying to get it under his coat, and I saw what was going on. There was only one thing to do, and Gates did it. He paid me a handsome sum to keep quiet and leave the school, and I did it. At that time I was very poor, and the money which I earned in such an easy manner came in mighty handy. But as years went on I found it wasn't easy. The thing weighed me down, and today I'm glad to get it off my chest."

"But why in the world should Gates have stolen his own cup?" asked Don.

"That I don't know; I can't help you there, Mr.——"

"Mercer," supplied Don.

"Mr. Mercer, that you must learn from someone besides me. I don't know. I only know that he paid me to keep quiet and to leave. He even got me a good job here in Ashland. But after a while I bitterly regretted the fact that I had ever seen him come out of the room, and I hated myself for taking the money. Dishonesty is a heavy, dragging burden, Mr. Mercer."

"It must be," Don admitted, dazed at his success. "But you needn't regret the fact that you saw Gates come out of that room. If you hadn't, we would never have found out that Arthur Gates took the cup, and Long would never have been cleared. As it is now we can clear him."

"How about me?" demanded the man. "Am I to be dragged into the light at this late day? Can't you cover me up some way?"

"I don't know," said Don, frankly. "I think that before we ever clear Long we'll make a great effort to find out why Gates took his own cup. If we don't things will be pretty cloudy. Tell me this, have you ever heard of or from Gates since?"

"No, and I never made any effort to. When he paid me my money and got me the job I had nothing further to do with him. As I told you before, I was in pressing need of both the money and the job, but now, as I look back, I'd sooner have been poor and at the same time honest. That is all I can tell you about it, Mr. Mercer, but I'm glad to get that off of my chest."

Don rose to go. "I sincerely thank you, Mr. Mulford. I think I can see how we can clear up everything without involving you any further. I guess if we go to Gates and tell him what we know he will be glad to confess without allowing any such disgraceful story to get into the newspapers. He is a very prosperous businessman now, and he would be willing to keep things quiet." He extended his hand and Mulford shook it.

"Good luck to you, Mr. Mercer, and whatever you do in life, keep away from anything shady," the former janitor said, in parting.

The daughter of the man came in at that moment and at her father's command she showed Don to the door. He went directly to a restaurant and ate a hearty supper, turning the amazing disclosure over and over in his mind. Before very long he was again on the train.

"Well, this is turning into a royal mystery," he reflected on the way back to school, "I certainly would like to know why Arthur Gates should have taken the trouble to steal the very cup which was to be turned over to him!"

Chapter 4
A Visit to Mr. Long

Don allowed Sunday to go by without saying anything to the colonel about the cup and the story attached to it. He had already told it all to his brother and Terry, and they spent fruitless hours trying to figure out why Gates had stolen his own cup.

"Beats me," Jim finally confessed, giving it up in despair.

"It is something like that old story of the man who stole his own wedding present," suggested Terry. "Only, that fellow had some plan in mind when he did it. He wanted to stop the wedding."

"Arthur Gates had some scheme in mind, don't doubt that," Don said, seriously. "But what was it?"

On Monday he told his story to the colonel. The headmaster was astonished and in one sense pleased.

"Then Long is innocent!" he exclaimed. "That's splendid! My former cadet comes out with flying colors!"

"But another one does not!" Don reminded him.

"Well, yes, that is so," admitted the colonel. "But still I would rather see it the way it is than to have to think George Long is guilty. Not that I wish to see either or any of my boys guilty of dishonor, but what I mean is this: Long was such a fine clean fellow that it hurt to think that anything was wrong with him. Gates, on the other hand, was not so straightforward. I can't even say that he was dishonest, but he was less frank than the cadet captain."

"I see what you mean." Don nodded. "But now we will have to admit that Gates was dishonest, for he allowed the blame to settle on Long and never said anything about it at all."

"That is so," the colonel said. "What do you propose next? Shall Long be told of the story?"

"Privately, yes," Don replied. "But suppose we keep it rather quiet for a time? We do want to find out just why Gates took it, and a significant story may underlie his reason. My plan is to have a regular committee go and call on Mr. Long!"

"To see if he can add anything to the facts gathered?" the

23

colonel asked.

"Yes, just that. It may be that he has since found out something that will help. It won't do any harm to try. Do you know where he is living?"

"The last time I wrote to him he was living in White Plains. I'll give you his address and you can write and ask for an appointment."

"Do you think that is wise?" Don asked.

"Why not?"

"Well, he may still be hurt at the way the whole thing was received years ago and tell us very briefly but politely that he will not be at home to us. My plan is to drop in on him some evening and then he will have to receive us."

After thinking it over the colonel agreed that Don's plan was best and they decided on a committee. As they desired to keep the thing as quiet as possible it was finally agreed that Don, Jim and Senior Cadet Captain Hudson should do the calling on George Long. As soon as lessons were over Don hunted up the cadet captain and told him what was in the wind.

He was deeply interested and when Jim found that he was to be part of the committee his joy was great. Terry was slightly disappointed, but felt that he would eventually have some part in things. At least, he would hear how things turned out, and that in itself served to comfort him.

It was one night during the following week that the three cadets composing the committee arrived in White Plains. They started early in the afternoon and it was nearly eight o'clock when they arrived in the city. Their first step was to go into a drugstore and look up the name of George Long.

"Here it is," the tall senior captain said, pointing the name out to his companions. "He is still living at the address that the colonel gave us. Now, if he is at home we'll be in luck."

After some inquiry they found the street and half way down it a neat white house. There was a light in the living room and sounds of a radio could be heard as they stood on the front porch. Hudson touched the bell and they waited.

"Here's hoping he won't throw us out," whispered Jim.

"He won't," Don promised. "Not when I tell him what I have learned."

A very pleasant looking man in his early thirties opened the front door and turned on the front porch light. His face was thoughtful and he carried himself with an erect carriage that revealed his military training. In unconcealed astonishment he surveyed the three trim-looking cadets in their gray uniforms and gray overcoats. Quickly his eyes flashed to the W. M. I. on their hats and he knew that they came from Woodcrest Military Institute. His face was a study.

"Are you Mr. George Long?" asked Don, whom the others had agreed would be the spokesman of the party.

"Yes, I am," the man responded. "Won't you step in?"

The three cadets stepped inside a comfortable hall, removing their hats and loosening their overcoats as they did so. Long continued to look fixedly at them.

"We have come to see you on some very important business, Mr. Long," said Hudson, as there was a slight pause.

"Come in the living room," Long invited, leading the way. It was evident that he was deeply puzzled and fighting to get a grip on himself.

As they entered the living room, a neat, vigorous lady of about the same age as Long got up quickly from an easy chair in which she had been sitting. She looked from the cadets to her husband.

"If it is on business, George, I'll leave you to yourselves," she began, but Don quickly interrupted her.

"Please do not go," he said. "I am sure you will be quite anxious to hear what we have to say to Mr. Long. Before we go any further I want to introduce my companions and myself. This is Senior Cadet Captain Hudson, and this is my brother, Mr. Mercer. I am Donald Mercer, of the third class at Woodcrest."

"I'm glad to know you," Long said, having regained some of his composure by this time. "This is Mrs. Long. Won't you be seated?"

He turned off the radio music and they all sat down, the Longs expectant and the cadets cool. Don spoke slowly and calmly.

"Mr. Long, we have come to ask you to tell us what you know about that unfortunate affair of the Gates trophy of 1933."

A sudden dark look passed over the man's face and his eyes blazed. His voice had lost its friendliness when he spoke again.

"I had hoped you weren't here to talk about that," he said, excitement in his tone. "I won't answer a single question. I never was a thief!"

The three cadets sat unmoved and Don went on unevenly. "It was thought by a great many that you were, and it is still thought. There are very few persons in the world who know that you never were, but before very long everyone will know it. I think you will answer questions, Mr. Long, and willingly so, since it will help us to solve the whole mystery of that cup."

Mrs. Long was sitting up eagerly in her chair and her husband was staring. "Do you mean to say that you have found out anything about that cup?" Long asked, eagerly.

"I found out several things," Don answered. "But I think the wisest thing would be to hear what you have to say first. It may help us a lot, and then we'll tell you what we know. You may save yourself most of the details, for Colonel Morrell, who has always believed in you, has told us most of them."

"I know that the colonel has always believed in me, and I'm mighty proud of the fact," Long said. "Well, gentlemen, I must first beg your pardon for my outburst. The subject has long been a deep hurt to me, so you can understand just how I felt."

"Perfectly," nodded Hudson, the others assenting.

"Well, you know that the Gates cup was turned over to me and that it disappeared on the day of the presentation. I'm afraid that is all there is to it. I was accused by the senior Gates, but generously protected by Arthur."

A swift glance passed between the cadets, a glance which the Longs noticed and wondered at. Don again took the lead.

"Are you sure you have told us everything, Mr. Long?" he asked, looking directly into the former cadet captain's eyes. "Can't you tell us why you went around so glumly after Gates won the chance to compete against Roxberry, and again in the same manner after he had won against that school and had claimed the highest honors? It looked to everyone then as though you were jealous, but we have a feeling that there was something else. Suppose you tell us now."

Long hesitated, and his wife reached over and touched his arm. "George, you must tell everything to these boys. I know that you consider it honorable to keep quiet, and that you have done so for all of these years during which you have been cruelly misjudged, but I think it is high time you made some effort to clear yourself."

Long came to a decision. "Very well, boys. I'll tell you

everything. Perhaps I've been foolish to keep it all to myself in this way, but I've thought it the honorable thing to do. The reason I looked so glum at the time Arthur Gates won in the competition examinations and later again Roxberry, is simply because Gates won them dishonestly!"

"Both of them?" asked Jim sharply.

"Yes, both of them! Copied his answers out of textbooks for the elimination and later bribed a professor from Roxberry on the big examination! His money did it, and the professor mentioned gave him a complete list of the questions to be answered before the interscholastic contest. No wonder he won hands down!"

"How did you learn this?" Don asked.

"I knew, judging by our class records, that I should have defeated Gates in the eliminations. But I didn't say anything until he won the big event with one hundred per cent. Then, on the night that I first placed that cup on my dresser, I pinned him down to the facts and made him confess that he had stolen the entire thing. Gates was always rather weak and he admitted it readily, even telling me the methods employed.

"As you can imagine, I was utterly appalled. We were always a school noted for our cadet spirit and our honor, and it had been literally smeared by Gates' hideous act. The next day he was to step up on the platform and take a cup that belonged to another school, or at least one which he had not won cleanly, and he was going to do it with a smile on his face. Boys, I'm no cry-baby, but I did cry a bit then for the utter hopelessness of a man who would do that. Now I know where I was wrong. I should have dragged him to the colonel or have beaten the life out of him, but I thought I knew of a better way. I talked for two solid hours to him about honor and then left him alone in my room, after he had promised to write down a confession and stand clean. It wasn't an easy thing to do on his part, but he agreed, and he said he'd write it where it would be eternal and there would be no mistake about it. I didn't understand that, but I went outside for a walk, to cool off in the fresh air.

"And on the next morning the cup was there, but it later disappeared. He stepped up to the platform and took all the honors, and that knocked the theory I had held in the head. I thought that he had had the trophy stolen in order that he wouldn't have to accept it, thinking that he'd back out altogether. But he didn't. As I said before, he was mighty generous about it all, but of course, he had to be. He knew I was in a position to grind him to powder with a word, and he acted accordingly. I think that is the only reason his father didn't prosecute me."

"The story gets blacker each time we hear it," murmured Hudson.

"That explains a whole lot," Don said. "Now, I'll tell you what we know." He began at the point where he had read the notice of the resigning janitor in the issue of the *Bombardment* and told it to the finish. "So you can see, Mr. Long, that Gates stole his own cup. I guess he did it so as not to have to accept it."

"Perhaps he was brazen enough to accept all of the praise, but the cup was too much for him, and he knew he could not face that," Mrs. Long suggested.

"And yet that doesn't make it any the less dishonorable," Jim interposed.

"You still think there is some other reason for taking his own cup?" asked Long.

"I'm afraid so," confessed Jim. "Simply taking the cup, and still accepting all of the honors doesn't seem logical."

They talked on for some time, the Longs delighted at the good fortune which had come to them. It had grown so late that the cadets knew they could not return to the school that night. They talked of going to a hotel but the Longs promptly vetoed the suggestion, declaring that they could and would put them up for the night.

The cadets gladly accepted the invitation, and knowing that they were in no hurry, spent a happy evening with the Longs. Now that some of the bitterness was lifted from his mind George Long talked freely of the days during which he had been in the school.

"For the time being nothing will be said publicly," Don told Long, as they were leaving the next day. "We are not yet satisfied as to why Gates took the cup and we mean to make an effort to find out. In time, however, you will be completely cleared."

"With as many of them as are still alive," said Long quietly. "Some of them were killed in the war. I was in the war, too, and it is just by the mercy of the Almighty that I am not resting there now."

With the thanks and good wishes of the Longs echoing in

their ears, the three cadets left and were soon on the way back to Woodcrest.

Chapter 5
The Alumni Dinner

"I don't know whether this case gets better or worse as it goes on," remarked the colonel, after Hudson, Don and Jim had told him Long's story.

"As far as the proposition of clearing Long is concerned, it's turning out just right," Hudson remarked.

"That's right," the colonel agreed. "But now I find that Woodcrest didn't win the interscholastic scholarship contest at all. In time the truth will have to be made known and then we will receive an additional black eye."

"Perhaps not, sir," Don put in. "When the professor from Roxberry who sold the examination to Gates is known they may wish to keep it quiet. There is no way of telling just how it will all turn out."

"Maybe so," the colonel replied. "Now, let me tell you what I plan to do. In about three weeks I am going to have the first alumni dinner in Clanhammer Hall, when we will change the name of the place to Alumni Hall. I am going to write to Arthur Gates to attend that affair and while he is here we'll see if there is anything to be learned about the events of the past. Gates has never attended an alumni dinner before, possibly because he has feared to meet Long at one."

"Then how will you get him to attend this one?" Jim asked.

"I'm going to write and tell him that as this is the most important meeting that we have ever had it is absolutely necessary that we have the winner of the interscholastic contest with us." The colonel's face became suddenly red and his gray eyes glinted dangerously. "I'm sorry to think that I'll have to shake hands with him and pretend that he is the same as any other man, but that is the only thing I can do under the circumstances. It is all important that George Long be cleared and that we find out why Gates took that cup. That is as much as we can do right now, and I'll let you know when something new turns up."

They left the colonel then and for the next week very nearly forgot the affair of the cup. They were now in the full swing of their school life, enjoying it as never before. Both Don and Jim were on the football squad, and although they were not permitted to play in every game they did get some part in most games. The red-headed boy was still with the track, rapidly making a name for himself as a fast and steady runner.

At the end of a week the colonel called Don and the senior cadet into his office. He had a letter in his hand.

"I just received a reply to my letter," he stated. "Arthur Gates will be here on the night of our alumni dinner. He writes to say that he has never had the opportunity to come before, but that he'll be very glad to come and help open Clanhammer as the new Alumni Hall. That's very nice of him, I'm sure. If he knew what we know, he wouldn't come near the school."

"That's true," nodded Don. "What are your plans for the evening?"

"I haven't decided as yet," the headmaster admitted. "But I shall want you and Hudson and Jim to be in the room and watching Gates. I am going to ask most of the seniors to act as waiters, and I'll see to it that you and Jim are on the table with Gates."

On Monday of the following week a corps of carpenters and painters swooped down on old Clanhammer Hall and went to work. In between periods and after school the cadets watched them with interest. Old and rotting boards were ripped off and new ones put in their places, old paint was scraped and in a short time the old building stood out in glowing splendor. Leaves were raked up and broken windows replaced. The hall was completely transformed.

On the inside the work was even more thorough. Old benches were torn out, one or two old partitions followed, and the entire left side of the original school was turned into a huge dining hall. In the days of its infancy Clanhammer had had a small dining room, because enrollment had been small there. Now two classrooms joined with that original room made up the new and spacious alumni dining room.

Upstairs was left pretty much as it had been and then the new furniture was moved in. Long tables and plenty of chairs composed the new equipment, and in a few days the new sign, Alumni Hall, was painted over the front door.

A number of seniors had been chosen as waiters and Don and Jim had been told to join them. On the night of the dinner they assembled early in the kitchen of the hall and began preparations. The kitchen had been refitted and at present was full of steam and the odors of half a dozen foods. The cooks had their hands full watching the restless cadets, who sampled the food at every opportunity.

"I'm warning you," shouted Pat Donohue, the chief cook, as he wiped the perspiration from his red face. "The next fellow I see dipping bread in the gravy will catch a frying pan back of his ears! Don't you boys never get fed during meal times?"

"No, Pat," said one of the seniors, gravely. "Your food is so good that we never get enough of it! Don't blame us for snitching a little now and then, for it is out of this world!"

"Humph," snorted the cook, suspiciously. "That sounds fine, but I got a sneaking suspicion you just said it to make me feel good. Get your fingers out of that salad!"

"Isn't there anything we can have without being jumped on for it?" demanded Hudson.

There were a half dozen rolls which had fallen into some heavy grease earlier in the evening. They were now on a plate nearby and the grease did not show. Pat pointed to them.

"There's some fine rolls that you can have," he said, a twinkle in his eye. A dozen hands reached for the rolls and the lucky ones began to eat hastily. But in a minute there came a chorus of protesting cries.

"What in the world did you put in these rolls?" gasped a senior, as he tasted the grease.

"Who, me?" asked Pat, innocently. "I didn't put nothing in 'em. I guess they was that way when they came. I dunno, I haven't tasted 'em."

After that the cadets let the food alone. By this time they could hear the old graduates coming in, and soon the old hall echoed and re-echoed to the talk and laughter of the old students. From time to time the alumni wandered within sight of the busy corps of waiters, and then the cadets got a glimpse of them.

Working busily the cadets soon had the supper on the table and then the graduates marched in, the old-timers in the lead and the others following.

Just before they sat down the colonel beckoned to Hudson and spoke to him in a low tone. "The man at my right is Arthur Gates," he said. "Not on this table, but on the second table. Just watch him closely and see what his reaction is to any announcement about class trophies."

Hudson nodded and carried the message to Don and Jim. The meeting opened with a word of thanks by the colonel and then with a noisy scraping of chairs the old cadets sat down. It was now a busy period for the young waiters. They walked rapidly from the kitchen to the dining room, putting on the food, replenishing the supply of rolls, and seeing to it that everyone was well served.

It was during a pause between courses that Don and Jim got their first real look at Arthur Gates. He was sitting at the end of the second table, conversing with some of his old class-mates. He was stout and pale, wore glasses and had very little hair on his head. His eyes were shifty and they decided, even discounting what they knew about him, that they did not like him.

After the final coffee cups had been cleared away several speeches were made. They recalled the earlier days of the school, when the colonel was a very young man, and one of them told of mistaking him for the janitor.

Eventually Gates was called upon and the three boys listened to him in amazement. He spoke of the glorious year in which the school had won the cup and seemed not in the least abashed.

Jim whispered to Don, "I'll be doggone glad when we can produce proof and show that fellow up. Can you imagine a guy like that taking credit while Long is in disgrace?"

"I won't mind spiking his guns," whispered Don indignantly, in return.

Gates concluded his speech in a burst of handclapping, in which the colonel did not take part. The headmaster rose slowly and addressed the gathering.

"I have a very pleasant surprise for you, gentlemen. During the last few months I have had a committee of my boys look through the school for the trophies of former years. They have recovered every one of them, and in a very short time I shall show them to you. Every one, gentlemen."

The three cadets looked quickly at Gates. He was paying strict attention to Colonel Morrell and his face had become very pale. Nervously his hands crumpled the tablecloth.

"I have made over one room into a trophy room," continued Colonel Morrell. "In that room you will find the walls lined with the emblems which speak of the glories of the past, the standards for the winning of which you gave so much courage and loyalty. Cups, flags, banners, shields—all are there and in looking at them I am sure you will find many a stirring memory. I propose that we now go directly to the trophy room and look over the collection, and I challenge any of you to show me wherein we of the present day have left a single historic trophy out."

There was a pushing back of chairs and the graduates followed the colonel out of the dining room into a smaller room which had been beautifully decorated. The last glimpse that the three cadets had of Gates he was close on the heels of the colonel.

"I guess I see the colonel's point," whispered Hudson, as they prepared to clear the tables. "Wait until you hear what he has to say."

The next two hours were busy ones, as the cadets were compelled to clear all the tables, eat, and help stack away the piles of dishes. When they returned to the empty dining room they found that most of the guests had left the hall. After a time the colonel sought them.

"Did you observe anything?" he asked guardedly.

"Mr. Gates looked ill at ease when you said you had all of the trophies," Don answered.

The colonel nodded. "I watched him closely when we got into the Trophy Room," he said. "His eyes eagerly swept the room, and after that he seemed ill at ease no more. He saw that the class of 1933 cup was not there. But he must have known that it was not there in the first place."

"He must have the cup at home somewhere," said Jim.

"I believe he has. But listen while I tell you what happened. One of the graduates said, 'Too bad we haven't the interscholastic cup of 1933.' There was a dead silence and then Gates said, 'Let's forget that altogether, fellows.' I guess he would like everyone to forget about that cup."

"No doubt," agreed Hudson. "Well, what is the next move?"

"Let's wait awhile," answered the colonel. "I had a talk with Gates and he told me that he and his family were about to move here to Portville to live! That may mean something definite in the future."

Chapter 6
Added Mystery

A number of cadets, clad in the regulation football pants, and blue and white jerseys of Woodcrest football team ran swiftly around the track back of the school. It was the custom of Coach Briar to give his men a single lap around the field after a strenuous workout, and the team was winding up for the day. Don and Jim held their place well in the front with the leaders.

The lap completed they rushed down the steps that led into the basement and with a series of wild whoops piled into the locker rooms. A hissing sound announced that the showers had been turned on, and a film of steam vapor spread rapidly over the room. Jerseys came off on the double and more than one helmet rolled unheeded across the dusty floor.

Coach Brier walked in slowly and looked with approval at his charges. They were in fine condition and had won every game of the season. At no time in the year had they been in any danger of losing, and the fighting spirit was more than gratifying to the athletic coach.

The tumult in the locker room increased with each passing moment. Half a dozen young huskies had found themselves stripped at the same time and a wild rush for the showers resulted. There was pushing and shoving and shouting, which would have disturbed the nerves of someone less stout in that respect than the popular coach. But he merely smiled and looked on, wisely confining his talk to football subjects.

"Only one more team to play, coach," shouted Quarterback Vench, of the third class. "We ought to be able to take them."

"Don't be too sure," warned the coach.

"We'll sure take one healthy crack at them," put in Douglas, who ran in the backfield for Woodcrest.

"Is there any chance of playing Dimsdale this year, coach?" cried Hudson, from the back of the room.

A look of gravity spread over the genial face of the coach. As if by magic the uproar in the room ceased. Hudson had struck a sore point.

In the past Woodcrest had played an annual game with Dimsdale, a preparatory school close by. The contest had been the big event of the whole fall season and the rivalry had been keen. But in recent years there had been no games between the two schools, owing to an unfortunate affair that took place after one of the games on the Woodcrest home field. At that time Woodcrest had defeated Dimsdale for five years straight, and in the game that followed the preparatory school had won. The fact went to the heads of the students of the rival school, and besides painting the 12 to 0 score on the side of the school with white paint they had ruthlessly broken windows and wrecked some school furniture. The cadets' battalion had formed and had given the rioters a severe beating, although they were supposed to merely chase them off the grounds. From that time forward there had been no games.

However, that had happened years ago and there was no thought that it would happen again. Each year the cadets clamored to play against Dimsdale and each year they were refused. As the years went on the situation became harder. Insolent Dimsdale scholars openly booed the cadets and the boast was common with Dimsdale students that the Woodcrest school was afraid to play them. In large bodies the Dimsdale rooters came to the cadet games and openly cheered for the rivals of the cadets, no matter who or what they were. It was as much as flesh and blood could stand, and to old veterans like Hudson and Barnes and Berry, the flashing backfield men, it was especially bitter to think that they must graduate without a chance to play their detested foes.

To Hudson's question the coach looked troubled. "I don't know, Hudson," he said. "You know what the attitude of Melvin Gates is."

Don stopped tying his shoe to look up. "What has Melvin Gates to do with it, coach?" he asked.

"Everything," responded the coach, gloomily. "It so happens that he is the chief trustee and that he donates the most money to the school. Although Colonel Morrell owns the school it is really run by a board of trustees, and the head trustee is Melvin Gates. He has never gotten over the affair of the last Dimsdale game, and he positively refuses to allow the school to play the other outfit. As he holds most of the power I suppose the colonel can't risk losing his support, so we have to go without our game each year."

"Is he the only one against it?" Jim asked.

"Yes," nodded the coach. "The only one."

Vench snorted in disgust. "Can you beat that? Just because something happened long ago he has to act like a spoiled baby about it! That's what I call fine, noble sportsmanship!"

"You don't know much about it," grumbled Hudson. "This is only your second year. Wait until you have had to swallow their insults for four years. Why, look at the Roxberry game, and what those guys did. Started yelling every time the signals were called, so that we couldn't get them. If I had my way I'd turn the whole corps loose to clean 'em off the field."

Young Major Rhodes, former cadet captain of the senior class and now chief drill instructor, drifted in just then. "I agree with Hudson," he said, quietly. "I had to put up with it for four years and then finally graduated without getting a chance to play against them. I think we've been wrong about the whole thing from start to finish. Suppose a delegation of you fellows go and see the colonel and tell him that the whole school wants to play Dimsdale."

"What good will that do?" asked Coach Brier.

"I don't know that it will," confessed Rhodes. "But I do know that there will be a meeting of the trustees on Friday and at that time the colonel can put it up to them again."

"And get turned down once more," snapped Berry, to whom Dimsdale was a nightmare.

Rhodes shrugged his broad shoulders. "I don't know, but you can at least try. Someday the break has got to be made, and the sooner the better."

"Do you think this year would be a good one to play Dimsdale?" inquired a substitute, timidly. "They are Class A champions, you know, and they have a powerful team."

"I wouldn't care how big their team is," declared halfback Barnes. "Just put me where I can rip holes in their line, that's all!"

The coach looked at the boys silently for a time. "All right, boys," he said. "I guess there is no harm in trying out Rhodes' suggestion. Suppose you three veteran backfield men consider yourselves a committee and approach the colonel on the subject. Let's see if we can get any action this year."

That night Don consulted earnestly with Jim and the result was a letter which he wrote to his father. After that they waited, with the rest of the school, for the decision of the trustees.

What the young substitute had said about Dimsdale was true. They were at present occupying the exalted position of champions of the Class A divisions, and they boasted a powerful, line-smashing team. In one sense it was not a wise year to start playing the old rivals again, for the Woodcrest team was small and fast, but in no way compared with the other school as far as bulk of players was concerned. But the cadets were mad clean through and did not hesitate to take on the other school, in anticipation at least.

The colonel received the committee of three and expressed with them the desire of renewing relations with the preparatory school. He promised to take the matter up with his board of trustees and see what he could do with the one obstinate member.

"It is time that Mr. Gates got over his prejudice," he admitted. "We'll see what we can do."

On the day of the trustee meeting Don received a letter from home and he and Jim read it over with satisfaction. Don nodded across the table to Jim as he finished it.

"I guess it won't make any difference which way the meeting goes now," he stated.

On the following day when the team finished their workout, the coach was not with them. He had gone into the school building to find out the result of the trustee meeting. The players stood around with sweaters and coats as protection against the sharp November wind. Before long they saw the coach come from the main hall and walk slowly toward them.

"Walks very slowly, something like a funeral march," observed Hudson, with a gloomy shake of his head.

When Brier reached them he did not waste any words. He shook his head and spread out his hands with a gesture that told the whole story.

"Same as ever, boys," he announced briefly. "Gates refuses to allow us to play Dimsdale."

Barnes and Berry took off their helmets at the same moment and slammed them on the ground viciously. Hudson turned away, a lump in his throat. His last ambition, that of playing against Dimsdale, was frustrated, and the fact hurt. Growls came from the rest of the squad. Vench gritted his teeth and sneered at the narrow-minded attitude of the chief trustee. Only Don and Jim kept silent, and as they were new members on the football team the fact was not noticed.

"That means giving it up for at least another year, I suppose," shrugged Rhodes.

"Maybe until Gates dies, I don't know," returned the coach.

"Blessings on him and all his money!" murmured Barnes, sarcastically.

After the customary lap around the field the boys went back to dress, annoyed and growling at the situation. It was not until they were in their own room that Don spoke his mind.

"Jim, I believe that there's something more to this than we can see on the surface," he said.

"What do you mean?" his brother asked.

"I mean that I don't think Melvin Gates is keeping us from playing Dimsdale simply because of the after-game riot of years ago. Why in the world should he be so particular? Every student wants to play and every trustee wants to let us, but still he holds out. I think there is some added mystery in it all, and that he has some deep and secret reason for not wanting us to play Dimsdale!"

Chapter 7
The Trustees' Meeting

On the following morning Don sought out the colonel and asked for a few minutes to talk over an important matter. At the colonel's invitation he sat down and came at once to the point.

"Colonel Morrell," he began. "You only tolerate Mr. Gates' attitude because he is the senior trustee and actually controls the school by his money, isn't that so?"

The colonel was astonished but he nodded frankly. "Yes, that is so. Of course, Mr. Gates has been a trustee for a good many years and there is something else to consider besides his money, but I'll admit that plays a big part. It costs something to run the school and his generosity has made a lot of things possible that we would otherwise have done without."

"Of course," responded Don. "Is his obstinate attitude confined simply to this matter of football, or does he make things unpleasant for you in other ways, Colonel Morrell?"

"In some other things he is very disagreeable, too," the headmaster said. "But in the matter of the football game he is unusually so. What makes you ask?"

"If you had someone else to take his place, who would advance as much money as he does, and with not nearly as much trouble, would you consider running directly against Mr. Gates?" Don went on, ignoring the colonel's question.

The colonel thought for a moment. "Yes, I think I would," he admitted, slowly. "As I told you before, Mr. Gates has made things pretty disagreeable for me on several occasions. He has a sort of stranglehold on the school simply because of his wealth and that makes it hard for the rest of the trustees and myself. In other words, if he wants a thing done his way he has only to say so and tap his pocketbook and we all have to do as he wants us to."

"That's just about what I thought," nodded Don. "Now, I'll tell you what I have in mind, Colonel Morrell. When I was home last summer I talked to my father quite a bit about the school and he shares my enthusiasm for it. When I heard of the trouble you had with Mr. Gates about the football situation I

40

wrote to him and asked him if Mr. Gates ever got disgusted and left the trustee body would he consider becoming a trustee in Gates' place, providing he was elected to the body. He wrote back and said that he would."

The colonel digested the news slowly. "That is very nice of your father and I certainly appreciate it," he said at last. "But of course I could not simply ask the senior Gates to resign so that I could put another man in his place."

"I wouldn't want you to do that," answered Don, quietly. "But this is what I mean. You know that the entire student body wants to play Dimsdale and that one man alone is holding us back. What I propose is this. Suppose a committee consisting of two representatives from each class waits on Mr. Gates and tells him plainly that the school is determined to play our rival? If he is unruly and threatens to resign we'll just allow him to resign and my father will take his place."

"I see now what you are getting at," cried the colonel. "We won't be driving him out, but he will be driving himself out! It will give us an opportunity to see if he is simply bluffing and at the same time you boys will get your game. Personally, nothing would suit me better than to see that game played. I think it is high time that the unfriendliness of years standing is done away with and that athletic and other relations be restored between this school and Dimsdale."

"Then you approve of my plan?" asked Don.

"I certainly do. The issue will then be squarely up to Mr. Gates and it will be up to him to decide what course to pursue. I won't have anything to say about it, nor will the other trustees, and if he wishes to resign your father will take his place. Nothing could be more clear-cut than that."

"When will there be another meeting of the trustees?" inquired Don.

"In three days' time. We did not get all business finished at the last meeting, due mostly to the football discussion, and we must meet again then."

It was agreed that Don should inform the captains and lieutenants of each class to appear before the trustees and explain their stand. After he had left the colonel's office he went to class and later hunted up the cadets whose presence would be required. All of them were instructed to keep things quiet until after the meeting of the trustees, and all agreed to do so.

On the night of the meeting the selected cadets were ready

and met outside the colonel's office. Hudson and Berry represented the first class, Douglas and Don the third. The trustees had arrived and were inside, settling themselves and talking.

The colonel opened the door and allowed them to march in, where they faced the slightly astonished trustees. They soon made out Melvin Gates, a tall, thin man with burning bright eyes and a lofty air about him. Colonel Morrell came briefly to the point.

"These cadets, gentlemen, represent the student body, and are here to speak for themselves. As you remember, at the last meeting it was decided that the school was not to play Dimsdale, now or ever, according to Mr. Gates. I passed that message on to the corps, but it seems that they refuse, for once, to accept the decision."

Melvin Gates straightened up in his chair and shot a bitter look toward the stalwart cadets. "Oh, they refuse to accept it, do they?" he said, in a rasping voice.

The colonel looked at Hudson, who spoke up in reply. "Yes, Mr. Gates, the student body refuses to accept the decision. We are taught good sportsmanship here at Woodcrest and the doctrine that men are to be met and treated like men. We feel that it is unfair to brand the Dimsdale school of today with the stigma of a set of rowdies of the past, so we are here to respectfully protest the ban against playing them."

"I don't care what you are here to protest!" shouted Gates, rising in excitement. "I have refused to give my sanction to this game, or to the proposition of renewing any kind of relations with Dimsdale school, and I will not retract one word of it."

"It is most unfortunate that you feel that way, sir," replied the senior Cadet Captain. "For we are going to play them as soon as possible!"

There was a gasp from the assembled trustees and Gates' face reddened. He snapped around on the silent headmaster.

"Morrell, are you going to allow this to go on?" he demanded.

"I do not see that I can do anything about it," said the colonel. "It is the fervent wish of the entire corps that we play Dimsdale, and I am heartily in favor of it myself."

"You know what this will mean to the school!" cried the angry Gates. "I will resign and withdraw every cent of my money."

"I should be sorry to see you do that, Mr. Gates," returned

the colonel. "But I am not going to thwart my boys any longer."

"All right, sir, all right," ground out the trustee. "Then I resign, at once! How will you manage to get along without my money, Morrell? Answer me that!"

"I beg your pardon, sir," put in Don. "But my father has agreed to become a trustee in your place if you should resign."

Gates was taken aback. A murmur arose from the other trustees and more than one satisfied look was exchanged. The chief trustee shook with rage.

"Oh, very well, gentlemen, very well! If that is the way you feel about it, I see that there is nothing left for me to do but to resign. This is a pretty cheap game to play, Morrell."

"It isn't a game at all!" retorted the colonel, with spirit. "How long do you suppose these young men were going to submit to the rule of one man on a question like this? Don't you see that for years you have made these young men the laughing stock of the neighboring preparatory schools, and that we have been questioned on all sides as to our sportsmanship? It was only a matter of time, Mr. Gates, and I was simply lucky enough to have Mercer's father offer to take your place if you resigned."

"Had it all planned out, eh?" snarled Gates. "Mercer's father prepared to step in as soon as I stepped out!"

"Yes, but you can't blame anyone if you want to step out," returned the colonel. "If you will resign, someone must take your place. We will receive your resignation at any time, Mr. Gates."

"You'll get it soon," the trustee promised. "Let me tell you, nothing good will come of all this. The idea of you young cadets wanting to play Dimsdale this year! Why, everybody knows that they will run away with you!"

The cadets flushed and Berry replied. "We will try hard to make them run after us, and not away with us, sir."

"They'll make a laughing stock of you!" shouted the irate trustee.

Colonel Morrell turned to his cadets. "You may go, boys," he said. "Spread the news that Woodcrest will play Dimsdale!"

The cadets saluted and left the room and in a short time the news was flying all over the school. The cadets went wild and the coach was enthusiastic. On the next day a formal challenge was sent to the rival school, and in another day the reply was received.

"We play 'em on November 24th," said the coach, briefly. "I hear that they plan to wipe up the ground with us!"

"That is what you hear!" smiled Hudson, grimly. "Wait until you see the game!"

Chapter 8
An Old Score Settled

A low, gray ceiling of clouds hung over the field at Wood-crest when the cadet team came out to play that November afternoon. Stands were crowded, and as the team entered the field a cheer went up from the Woodcrest section and a yell of derision from the Dimsdale side of the field. Briefly, the cadet team looked at the beefy Dimsdale team across the field, where they were running signals. Grim mouths, bright eyes, and hearts filled with determination marked the silent purpose of the young soldiers.

When the news of the coming game with the Class A champions had been circulated around town great had been the derision. The two teams were in different classes, the preparatory school ranking in the higher Class A division and the military school in the lighter Class B aggregation. Woodcrest had not lost a game nor had Dimsdale, in each class. Crushing power lay with the preparatory school machine and nothing but the stings of years of insults and determined purpose with the cadets. Those who cared for such things had made heavy bets against the cadet team and the feeling was general that Wood-crest was in for a bad beating.

The football coach had not said much to his team, but he had said just enough. He told them that the feeling was against their chances of winning, that the whole thing was looked upon as foolishness, and that Dimsdale was frankly considering it nothing more than a practice game. This was their chance, he told them, to settle once and for all an old score, and his only plea was that they play like gentlemen and forget revenge.

"Because if you think of it merely as a revenge, you are sure to lose," the coach wound up. "Bad sportsmanship spoils and defeats any game. Knowing you as I do and just how you feel, I know you'll play your hardest, and my only request is that you play clean and hard."

It was therefore a silent, grim group which trotted out on the gridiron and started to run through signals. Derisive yells and cat-calls came from the opposite side of the stands. They fell on heedless ears, or at least on unresponsive ones. Quarterback Vench called his signals quietly, the ball was snapped with calm accuracy, and although the hearts of the soldiers beat rapidly there was no outward sign to show that they were burning with an eager fire inside.

The cadet band struck up and played well, the cadets marching across the field to the grandstand side which they were to occupy. When they were seated the two teams began to take their places. Hudson, the Dimsdale Captain and the official met in the center of the field, the coin was tossed, and Dimsdale won the toss. They decided to kick and the teams lined up.

The ball was placed, the Dimsdale captain looked up and down his line to make sure that everything was ready. Tensely the cadets, spread out in receiving formation, waited. For an instant the field was in silence. Then, as both captains nodded, the referee blew his whistle sharply and the bitter game was on.

There was a thud as the ball was kicked and sailed in a long arc to the waiting arms of half-back Barnes. He tucked it under his arm securely and bounded off to the left side of the field. Realizing that he was in danger of outrunning his guards he slowed slightly and ranged himself behind Hudson, Berry and Vench. Behind this wall he ran the ball back to the center of the field before being downed. Lazily the preparatory players untangled themselves from the heap, but the cadets snapped into line with a spirit that showed their purpose.

Don and Jim were benched, as they were in nearly every game. In the following year, and their senior year they expected to play on the team regularly, but as yet they were only substitute. Jim played in the line in practice and Don had once or twice played halfback. Well wrapped in their heavy parkas they sat on the edge of the players' bench, wholly absorbed in the game.

Vench called his signals and the ball was snapped to Berry, who made five yards through tackle. It was apparent that Dimsdale was playing lazy football. The team was heavy enough to hold the cadets from any dangerous threat and that was all they were doing. The next two plays did not gain anything and Vench kicked out of danger. The ends got down under the ball and brought the Dimsdale captain to earth with a telling slam.

Dimsdale began a march which was alarming, but an accident changed the situation. Berry pounced on the ball when the right halfback fumbled it. Woodcrest was on the forty-five yard line and prospects were good.

"Those guys are playing awfully sleepy football," Don said to Jim. "Vench had better take advantage of it and get the ball across."

The same idea seemingly occurred to the little quarterback. He surveyed the team before him over the backs of his teammates and then suddenly bent down. Calmly and quickly his signals came.

The ball snapped back. Berry, Barnes and Hudson doubled up and ran toward the right side of the field, and the Dimsdale team swung in that direction. Vench, the ball buried deeply in his stomach, swung left and let loose all of his speed. For a moment there was a wild mixup on the right side of the line and then Dimsdale woke up, but too late.

Vench was away and down the field and the goal was close at hand. He crossed it with the nearest Dimsdale player three feet in back of him. A wild roar went up from the Woodcrest stand and the Dimsdale team looked bewildered. Vench was slapped and shaken by his enthusiastic teammates and then they prepared to kick the ball. The kick was made successfully and the score stood seven to nothing for Woodcrest.

Now, however, it was a different Dimsdale team that lined up for the kick. Energy took the place of indifference. Helmets were pulled on tightly, belts hitched, feet kicked ridges in the field and an aroused and dangerous foe faced the cadet team. But they found a wideawake outfit waiting for them, and the game went on with a punch. This time the prep school team drove forward with purpose and held the cadet team to four straight downs, Vench declining to kick.

When the ball finally passed to Dimsdale the drive began. The smaller team was not able to hold the Class A group. Steadily they stormed down the field until they were under the shadow of the goal and a touchdown seemed the only final result. It was then that a merciful break came to Hudson.

This game against Dimsdale had been Hudson's dream for years, and he was anxious to distinguish himself. His opportunity came with dazzling suddenness. Impatient at the time taken to put the ball over the goal line, and fearful that the half would end, for they were now in the second quarter, the Dimsdale quarterback called for a forward pass. The ball went to their left halfback, who tossed it like a bullet to the left end, hovering at that moment down near the goal.

Hudson had been slow to get away when the ball had been snapped and he was blaming himself for it, when he saw the ball come speeding through the air, over his head. He leaped into the air as though there were springs on his feet. The ball stopped in the cup of his hands and he landed, hesitated, slightly dazed, and then, with a bound that carried him forward, began to run up the field, to the opposite goal posts, which seemed miles and miles away.

A frantic roar burst from both stands and the Dimsdale players turned and threw themselves at him. One went down under his cleated feet and he avoided him, a second he straight-armed with no uncertain force and then he broke away on a long run. Chaos broke loose in the stands and the captain, his supreme chance with him and up to him, ran as he had never run before, to cross the goal line at top speed and touch the ball to earth amid a terrific uproar. The goal had barely been kicked before the whistle blew, ending the half.

Down in the locker room the coach was quietly encouraging. "You are doing splendidly, boys," he smiled. "It is hurting the pride of the A champions terribly to have a score of 14 to 0 against them. You can all see we owe the last score, with all due credit to Hudson's run, to the quarterback's error. They were sure to drive over the goal, but he made the mistake of tossing a pass, which Hudson speared. The next time they begin to drive, look out!"

The coach turned out to be a true prophet. Dimsdale received the kick-off in the second half and drove with crushing force right down the field and over the line for their first touchdown. The cadets were unable to hold them and the goal was kicked, making the score 14 to 7. The drive was accompanied by rough handling on the part of the heavier players, and two of the cadets were slightly injured and had to be replaced. Jim was sent in and played guard, while Don waited for his chance.

"Well, it's a cinch we'll never beat them at straight football," remarked Vench, as the quarter ended, the cadets failing to gain an inch either through the line or around the ends. "They roll over us like a steam roller! We'll have to hold them down somehow!"

But the cadets were unable to do so. Once more the

preparatory players drove the lighter players before them like grass and scored a touchdown. They failed to kick the goal and the score stood 14 to 13.

"They are going to drive again," murmured the coach, to a friend. "My boys can't hold them on a drive."

And drive they did. They punched holes yards wide in the lighter team's line, rolled over them in waves, and steadily forced them back. In one of these smashes Berry was hurt and was helped off the field. The coach looked over his players and nodded to Don.

"Go in for Berry, Mercer," he said, and was none too hopeful when he said it for Don's playing was not spectacular and the coach wished that he had a star just at that moment.

Don tossed aside his parka and ran on the field, grateful for a chance, but not at all glad that Berry had been crippled for the time being. He reported to the referee and then, pulling his helmet down over his forehead and tightly around his ears, took his place in the backfield and bent down to catch the signals.

Dimsdale lost the ball on downs and the cadets got it almost in the shadow of the goal posts. It looked very much as though the usual thing would happen, the failure to advance and the necessity of a kick to save themselves, or losing the ball right there. The ball was snapped and a scant two yards were made.

Don played an average, ordinary game, carrying the ball twice for short gains and playing his part as interference. He found himself opposed to one large player on the other side who began to rough him with unnecessary force. It was the right halfback, a heavy-set individual who threw all of his weight with paralyzing force on Don at every opportunity. Don made no complaint, because it was part of the game for the other fellow to drop him whenever possible, and for some time he tried to believe that the man was not stepping out of bounds, but before long he knew this wasn't so.

He carried the ball again and the same player tackled him, rolling him over and thudding down on him violently. The breath was knocked out of him and he wobbled slightly when he got up, but he said nothing, partly from a lack of breath and partly from a desire not to complain. But when the same man viciously dug him with his elbow he protested.

"Keep your elbow to yourself or I'll report it to my captain," he warned him.

"Aw, run and tell your mama, soldier boy!" was the derisive answer.

Don made no reply but his eyes blazed as he went back to the place he occupied. The next few plays were grim and hard-fought. The cadets had managed to make first down and still held the ball.

"Are you all right?" Vench said to Don, as they formed again.

"Yes, only that big circus wagon over there is roughing me every chance he gets!" snapped Don.

"They are all doing it," replied the plucky little quarterback, wearily. He had worked with all his strength and was ready to drop. He fumbled the ball on the next pass and it rolled away. Immediately, every available player sprang toward the ball, but luckily a cadet fell on it, saving it for his team.

"Three downs, eight yards to go," groaned the coach. "They'll never make it, and Dimsdale will make another march down the field. It won't even do any good to kick."

Don had run toward the rolling ball, to be met by his heavy rival and knocked flat. There was no excuse for it, as there had been no danger that he would recover the ball, but he went flying, nevertheless, to land with jarring force on his stomach. With his breath whistling through his set teeth he staggered to his feet and walked to Vench, his eyes burning.

"Let me run that ball!" he hissed in the quarterback's ear. "Just give me a chance to run that ball once!"

Chapter 9
Terry Engages in an Argument

Mr. Vench had passed the ball more than once to Don without anything spectacular having happened, but he was willing to do it once more. One look at the flushed face of his friend showed him that Don was mad clear through and that he could be counted upon to put at least as much of a punch into the play as anyone. Accordingly, after a brief nod and a sweeping glance over the two tense teams Quarterback Vench bent over the center.

"19-84-6-10-2" he called, and the ball was snapped to him. The play meant that Don was to take the ball through tackle and guard, on the right side of the line.

The long, tapering fingers of Vench rested lightly but firmly on the ball and he swung it on to Don, who was passing him on a dead run, his head down, his eyes alert. Don's eager hands swept the ball out of the quarterback's grasp and he hurled himself into the gap which his teammates had opened between guard and tackle. For a single moment there was utmost confusion and then the Dimsdale players became aware that he had the ball. Those who were still on their feet swung in toward him.

They met a fighting-mad young savage. The first man clutched at Don's flying legs, only to be hurled violently to one side like a piece of paper. A second lunged and felt his one hand slide off the halfback's jersey. Then, up in front of Don loomed the big, beefy bruiser who had aroused his anger. There was a determined look in this man's face as he lunged at the running back.

Straight as a ramrod Don's hand shot out in the approved straight-arm, to catch the player squarely in the face. His head went back suddenly and he was pushed to one side, to drop limply to the ground, surprised and stunned. He had met his match and had received the worst of it. Don swept on out into the open field and began a run that brought the stands to their feet. Past the two half backs, narrowly missed by the Dimsdale fullback, and running a nip and tuck race with the enemy fullback Don beat the nearest man over the goal line by inches and touched the ball to the ground as the exhausted Dimsdale quarterback fell over him.

A mighty roar went up that lasted for at least three minutes and in that period a try for a goal was made but the ball missed the uprights by inches. They were taking their places once more when the whistle blew, ending the game with the score standing at 20 to 13 in favor of Woodcrest.

To the Class A champions the defeat was a crushing one and they left the field utterly humbled. To the cadets, suffering under the insults and sneers of years, the victory was more than sweet, and the score caused special rejoicing. Don was made much of and the coach assured him of a star's position on the team in the following season.

"Nothing but pure fighting spirit won that game for you, boys," the coach told them in the locker room. "Those fellows could parade through you for a touchdown every time they wanted to, but it was your alertness, as typified by Hudson's catch of the forward pass, and your sheer determination, as Mercer showed, that took the game, not to mention the intelligent handling of the little quarterback. Man to man you were outplayed and outweighed, but you beat a mighty good team by courage and fighting spirit."

During the game Terry was engaged in an unexpected argument. It was the custom at Woodcrest when they had a game of any kind to place cadets at the entrances of the rival grandstand to direct people to their seats or to stop any horse play in the stands. As Terry was not on the football squad he was assigned to the task of standing guard at one end of the visitors' grandstand.

Terry did not mind in the least. He was dressed in his dress parade uniform and for the time being had a little authority, even though it was limited to bossing small boys and directing people to seats. There were enough girls in the stand near him to make him anything but sorry that he had on his best uniform, and he could see the game perfectly. Terry had no fault to find with his post.

Before the game started many couples and groups had passed him and entered the stands, picking their own seats, and the red-headed cadet did not move. He was only to pick seats when it became crowded, and not even then unless requested, so he contented himself with watching the people as they passed him and entered the stand. All of them were friends of the preparatory school team and they carried red banners with a black D on them. A number of young men sat very near where Terry was standing and they looked him over and made a few would-be funny remarks to which Terry paid no attention.

When the Woodcrest team trotted out some of the Dimsdale supporters booed it heartily and the blood rushed to Terry's cheeks. For the moment he regretted the fact that he was not on the football team and playing in today's game. Grimly he pictured himself smashing wide holes through the opposite lines and the prospect was pleasing. He decided that he had had enough of running and that on the next gathering of football candidates he would surely be there.

Something that was being said by the well-dressed youths near him attracted his attention at this point. One of them, in a plaid wool shirt and gray flannel slacks, was addressing a few of his friends.

"It's a wonder these soldier boys ever got up the nerve to play us," he announced. "Of course, it will be a walk-away with 'em. Alongside of our fellows they look like a kindergarten."

Terry rolled his head uneasily, much as though his collar was too tight and choking him. It was not his business to argue with visitors who might occupy the grandstand and he knew it. In the end, the score would speak for itself and it would be foolish to pick and bicker about it. Nevertheless, his one foot beat the boards of the grandstand flooring impatiently.

"What's been the matter with this cadet team for so long?" asked one of the boys. The lad in the plaid shirt took it upon himself to answer that.

"They've been afraid to meet us," he said, with conviction. "Those fellows haven't wanted to meet us, and I don't know what made them do such a foolish thing this year. Silliest thing I ever heard of."

This was too much for the red-headed cadet. He swung around on the group just back of him, at the same time pointing to the furry individual in the plaid shirt.

"Look here, mister!" he growled. "Let me correct you on one point. The student body of this school has been dying to get a crack at your school for years, in fact, for every year the games haven't been played. But I'll tell you why the games haven't been played. We have had a trustee named Gates who holds a grudge against Dimsdale because of some rough work they pulled off years ago when they won a game. While we had this trustee we couldn't play you, because he controlled the school, but he is gone now and that is why we're playing you."

"Well, that was pretty poor sportsmanship," protested the boy from the other school.

"Oh, I agree with you perfectly there," replied Terry, earnestly. "Very bad sportsmanship, but it happened. This year we purposely got him to resign in order to play you and resume athletic relations with your school. Maybe you'll win the game, and then again, maybe you won't, but I just didn't want you to go around with the idea that Woodcrest has been afraid to play you in the past."

With that Terry walked away, leaving the boys somewhat impressed. Terry noted that a man well along in years was looking at him as he walked down the steps and when Terry moved near him the man spoke.

"I heard what you said to those fellows," he said, nodding to the boys. "So it's been old man Gates who has kept the two schools from playing, eh?"

"Yes, he has kept bad feelings alive between the schools for a number of years," Terry replied. "But I guess that business is about over. I don't know why he had to be so bitter about it, but some folks hang onto a grievance like grim death!"

"Yes, and Gates is just that kind," nodded the man. "But I wonder if he hasn't got a good idea in doing it?"

"I don't know," Terry said. "What do you mean?"

"Did you ever know that Gates' son was put out of Dimsdale years ago for dishonesty?" the man asked.

Terry was instantly alert. "No, I never knew that. Young Gates went to school here, you know. Is that the same one?"

"Yes, Arthur Gates is the same one. He was put out of Dimsdale for dishonesty in his lessons at examination time when I went there, some years ago. I had no idea that it was Gates who was forbidding your school from playing against my Alma Mater, but now I think he must have been doing it deliberately, to keep you folks from knowing about his son."

"Yes, but that seems foolish," Terry argued. "It was hardly possible that anything would be said about his son."

"It might come out accidentally," the man said. "Or per-

54

haps Gates is sore at the school in general. I still believe that Gates did it intentionally."

So did Terry and for the next few moments he was so busy with his thoughts that he did not notice the people who passed him. In a few minutes the game began and he was lost in the details of the struggle. Great was his rejoicing when the cadet team put the ball over in the first quarter and at the groans which came from those beside him Terry chuckled gleefully.

And when Don crashed the line for his thrilling run down the field Terry's joy knew no bounds. He tossed his hat and cheered loudly. When the people began to pour from the stands he waited until the party of young men, now strangely silent, passed him. Then, in a voice like that of the young man in the plaid shirt he said: "Of course, it will be a walk-away with 'em. Alongside of our fellows they look like a kindergarten."

The young men looked around and Terry smiled. "Pardon me," said the red-headed boy. "Can you tell me who won the game?"

"Aw, go run around the lots!" snorted the leader, and Terry chuckled.

That night there was no studying done. A huge bonfire was kindled and until late they enjoyed themselves around it. The football team, held down to training for some weeks, was now allowed to break from the rules and eat something more sweet than substantial.

"And so that is why the Gates' have kept things at dagger points between the two schools, is it?" asked Don, when Terry told the events of the afternoon.

"Yes," nodded Terry. "Young Gates in particular seems to be a bird of very black feathers!"

Chapter 10
The Eagles Disappear

Colonel Morrell was interested when Don told him what Terry had learned. He had never known that young Gates had gone to Dimsdale.

"It seems that a lot is coming out concerning that man all at once," the genial headmaster remarked, running his hand through his gray hair. "Unfortunately, it does not happen to be of the best, either. I think I will write to the headmaster of Dimsdale and confirm that, because we don't want to pin anything on Gates if it doesn't belong there."

"No," admitted Don. "He has a bad enough name now, and there is no use in adding to it."

After the big game the school settled down to a few quiet days of normal routine. Now that the old and bitter score had been settled the cadets felt satisfied and they found that outsiders had a deeper respect for them. The lofty airs of Dimsdale students had quite vanished and the two schools looked forward to playing annual games.

The colonel informed Don that Terry's information was correct. "Professor Strong, the headmaster of Dimsdale, writes to say that Gates was a pupil there some years ago and that he was dismissed for dishonesty," the colonel said. "It appears very much as though his failings run along the one line."

On the following Wednesday after the big game a startling thing happened. A group of the cadets were talking around the door of the classroom when a cadet from Clinton Hall joined them. It was early in the day and none of the boys from Locke had been outside yet.

"What's the excitement, Apgar?" asked Jim noting the flushed face of the cadet.

"Didn't you fellows hear what happened last night?" the cadet cried. "The eagles are gone!"

"What? The eagles gone?" a dozen voices cried out.

"Sure, sawed right off at the base. Some of the fellows are out there looking at them now."

Instantly there was a wild rush for the front door of Locke

Hall. Interest and excitement ran high. The eagles referred to were two huge ornaments placed on the wide steps leading up to the main hall, and they had been donated to the school by an army officer who had learned his first military tactics at Woodcrest. They were made of hollow brass, stood four and one half feet high, and had looked bravely out across the campus for a number of years, a very real part of the makeup of the cadet school. They had always seemed immovable, and to be told that they had been carted off was a distinct shock to the young soldiers, to whom they were a source of intense pride.

Don, Jim and Terry reached the front steps as soon as any of the others and took in everything at a glance. The parapet of the steps looked strangely bare without the great brass birds, and the cadets hurried to look at the spot where they had stood. Sure enough, they had been sawed off close to the stone, and only an iron stem with some flakes of fillings remained to show where they had been.

"Now, who in the world could have done that?" gasped Hudson, looking about him in a dazed way.

"Whoever did it must have been awfully careful about it," ventured Berry. "It was done in the night and no one heard it, apparently."

"Somebody had better hunt up the colonel," suggested a cadet, and in a few minutes the headmaster was out on the steps, his face grave and thoughtful.

They kept a respectful silence while the colonel looked on the stone rampart and examined the rough stumps of iron upon which the eagles had been mounted. He then looked over the assembled cadets.

"None of you gentlemen heard any sound of sawing during the night, did you?" he questioned.

None of the cadets had heard anything. By this time almost the entire corps had assembled. Barnes reminded the colonel that the previous night had been a very dark one.

"True," nodded the colonel. "It looked like a storm and I remember that there was no moon and no stars. Well, this is a pretty serious business, boys."

"It's a pretty small kind of a trick," growled Hudson.

"We'll have to get to the bottom of it as soon as possible," the colonel went on. "No clues as yet, eh?"

"Here is one!" cried Lieutenant Thompson, suddenly straightening up. He had bent down, looking around the ground just beyond the steps. They all looked curiously, to see that he held a small red book in his hand. The colonel took it and looked it over, and a gasp went up from those nearest him.

"A Dimsdale year book, eh?" boomed the colonel.

It was indeed a small instruction book with the words "Dimsdale School" printed across the cover. A murmur of understanding went up from the students.

"A little revenge for the football defeat," cried Vench, voicing the sentiment of all of them.

"It looks very much like it," nodded the colonel, pocketing the book. "A very unfortunate way to feel, to put it mildly. I'm glad you found that book, Thompson, though I'm sorry it had to be just the way it looks."

Before anything more could be said the class bell rang out and the cadets started for their classes, talking it over between them. Vigorous resentment was felt against the rival school.

"Too bad those fellows have to be such poor sports," growled Terry, as a group of the third class men made their way down the hall.

"They can't seem to take defeat graciously or even without crying about it," Don said, regretfully.

"Did you fellows see the date on that rule book?" Jim asked.

"No, what was the date?" Vench asked.

"I was near enough to see it plainly. It had 1938 on it. Isn't that a pretty old rule book for a Dimsdale student to be carrying?" Jim asked.

"It does seem odd, if you look at it that way," Don assented. "You are sure it was a 1938 book?"

"Oh, yes. I saw it at close range."

The school buzzed with the news all day and knots of cadets talked it over from every angle. The colonel was unusually silent and in the late afternoon he sent three seniors as a committee to Dimsdale to protest and lay the matter before the school authorities there. When they came back there was a session with the colonel and then more and eager talk around the building. Hudson had been on the committee and he entertained a big group in his room just before study period. The cadets stood around or sat on his bed and drank in his words.

"The headmaster there was pretty well put out about it all," the senior captain told his audience. "He looked through the book and was unable to identify it as the property of any of the students. Did you guys know that the book was an old 1938 one?"

Some of them knew it. Hudson went on: "Professor Strong said that to his knowledge there is not a 1938 instruction book in the school, and he doesn't know of a single student who has a book as old as that. He expressed his regret that such a thing happened, but he does not believe for a minute that Dimsdale fellows did it. The only thing that makes it look bad is the fact that they lost that game last Saturday and of course it looks exactly as though they were out for revenge and took it out on our eagles. The student council over there is going to take up the matter and push it hard, because it looks bad for the whole school."

"I hope they didn't have anything to do with it," Berry declared promptly. "I hope the little book was just a plant, because I hate to think those fellows are such downright poor sports. But, as you say, it looks bad in the face of the past game."

"We'll all have to do a little detective work from now on," Barnes suggested. "Let's see if we can't find someone who met suspicious characters around here on that night, or something that will give us a clue."

"It might be a good stunt to go over to Dimsdale and rummage around in their boathouse or the sheds back of the school," a senior said, but the majority were against that.

"Not right now," Hudson declared. "That would be the surest way to start trouble. Let's wait until something more definite than that little book points to Dimsdale as the guilty party. We all think somebody from that school took the eagles, but until we have positive proof we'll give 'em the benefit of the doubt."

"But isn't it funny that no one heard them cut the eagles off?" asked Vench.

"I wouldn't say so," Thompson replied. "You see, they were cemented into the stone by a single rod. Now, it was no trouble at all to slip a thin metal saw in between the base of the eagles and the stone and saw through. An iron saw doesn't make much noise and it probably didn't take much time. Whoever did it knew just how to go about it."

There the matter rested for the time being, but the cadets continued to wonder and speculate. The student council of the rival school met and presented a resolution that they believed the students of Dimsdale to be not guilty in the matter of the theft of the brass eagles. Professor Strong talked with the colonel by telephone and informed him that he could not find a 1938 rule book in the institution nor could he find a single student who had a book as old as that. Further check, which was fairly accurate, revealed the fact that every Dimsdale boy had been in his room on the night of the mysterious affair, though there was nothing to show that some few students might not have sneaked from the building after lights were out. All these facts made some impression on the more thoughtful cadets, but it was not enough to make them feel altogether sure that the rivals had no hand in the affair.

"Too bad about it all," sighed Don. "Just when the relations between the schools were being mended so nicely! But we've simply got to find those eagles."

"Yes," Terry agreed. "No one has found out a thing, as yet. Apparently no one saw any suspicious characters around on that night and nothing has been learned down in the town. I'm afraid we'll have to look further afield for them."

On the following day Jim showed a dispatch from the weekly town paper to some of the cadets. Under an editorial heading, entitled "The Revival of Ancient Rowdyism," there followed a long article about the notoriously poor sportsmanship of Dimsdale.

"See who the author is?" Jim asked as they pored over the dispatch.

"The editor, of course," said Douglas.

"No," Jim denied. "Look at this passage." He read it to them all. "'A prominent citizen of this town, one of the newest and most influential of our local citizens, tells us that he is not in the least bit surprised at the turn things have taken. This citizen, formerly a trustee at Woodcrest, has stood out for years past as unalterably opposed to the resumption of relations between the two schools, having had occasion years ago to witness more than once the regrettable lack of honor and sportsmanship on the part of Dimsdale students. It is altogether too bad that young men, growing up in institutions of this kind, where they are fitting themselves to take an active part in the affairs of life, should have so little respect for the principles of decency and honor.'"

"Now, who wrote that?" Jim challenged.

"The editor," said Don. "But Melvin Gates stood at his elbow when he did it."

"I can't understand it," Vench said. "He certainly seems determined to keep alive bad feelings between the schools."

"All in all, that editorial is quite unfair to Dimsdale," Hudson declared. "Maybe a few fellows from that school did saw off the eagles, but there was no occasion to slam the whole school that way."

When Don, Jim and Terry were alone in their room Don said, "Melvin Gates is taking an awful chance by writing, or being party to the writing of, such a piece as that. What is to hinder someone from coming out and telling the truth about his son?"

"Perhaps he figures that if they did, Woodcrest people would naturally take his part against Dimsdale. I wonder if you fellows are getting the same idea that I am?" Jim advanced.

"Perhaps we are," Terry replied, slowly. "Are you beginning to think that Gates had the eagles stolen to keep alive bad feeling and to make us think he was right all along?"

"That is just what I think!" said Jim. "Just a sort of a petty revenge. Now all we have to do is to prove it!"

Chapter 11
The Hunt in the Swamp

"Guess what I just found?" smiled Cadet Jim Mercer, joining a group at the piano in the recreation room.

Douglas was playing the piano and Don, Terry, Vench and Hudson were standing around listening. Jim had been at Inslee Hall visiting a friend and had just popped into the recreation room. It was in the evening just before study period.

"The pot at the end of the rainbow!" laughed Vench. "Lot of people been hunting for that a long time!"

"I wouldn't be likely to find that at night, would I?" retorted Jim. He unbuttoned the overcoat and dipped his hand into his jacket pocket. "This is what I found."

He produced a long, thin instrument of steel, at the sight of which the assembled boys cried out. It was nothing less than a steel saw, slightly rusty from exposure to the weather. One end of it had been broken off.

"Ah, ha!" cried the senior captain, examining it closely. "A steel saw! That thing was used to saw off the base of our eagles!"

"No doubt about it!" murmured Douglas.

"And that isn't all," Jim went on, turning it over. "See the name on the other side of it?"

Stamped into the steel was the name "Henry Rose." They looked puzzled, and Jim went on to explain.

"Henry Rose is the name of the maker of the steel saw. All we have to do is to find out which hardware store in this town, or in an adjacent town, sells Henry Rose saws. That ought not to be hard."

"No," agreed Terry. "Where did you find it, Jimmie boy?"

"In the grass at the end of the campus. I took a short cut across from Inslee and my foot struck something in the grass. I wouldn't have paid any attention to it, only it flew across the grass with a zipping sort of a sound and it aroused my curiosity. So I picked it up, and when I saw what it was I knew it must have been part of the game."

"Shall we show it to the colonel?" asked Don.

"Not right away," advised Hudson. "Tomorrow is Saturday and we have half day off. Suppose we fellows go down to Portville and do a little snooping on our own account. We may be able to scare up a clue or two."

"That sounds reasonable," Jim nodded. "There is only one hardware store in town, so we shouldn't have any trouble."

On the following afternoon the six cadets entered the hardware store of John J. Potts. Mr. Potts himself, a little, energetic man, bustled up to them, rubbing his hands.

"Hello, boys," inquired Mr. Potts. "What can I do for you today? I have nothing in the way of swords or bayonets, but perhaps you'll want something more useful, a can opener, for instance."

Having delivered himself tactfully of his feeling toward war and the implements of war, Mr. Potts laughed and the cadets smiled pleasantly. Mr. Potts was harmless and they knew it. Jim showed him the broken blade and the others watched him closely.

"Do you keep Henry Rose steel saws?" Jim asked.

Mr. Potts took the saw, examined it, and nodded. "Yes, I do. Nice blade, just the right play and solidity to it, retails for—"

"Never mind that," Jim cut him short, sensing Mr. Potts' desire to talk at length. "Have you sold any lately?"

"I sold three of them to Peter Cozoza last week," replied the Storekeeper, promptly.

"When was it?" Vench asked, eagerly.

"Last Monday," Mr. Potts supplied. The cadets exchanged glances.

"Who is Peter Cozoza?" Hudson put in.

"He is a laborer, lives over on Meadow Street, out by the swamps."

"He didn't say why he wanted them, I suppose?" Don inquired.

"Oh, no," protested Mr. Potts. "And of course I didn't ask him. I'm not in the habit of asking people what they buy things for, you know!"

"I know it!" returned Hudson, gravely. "You wouldn't do anything like that, Mr. Potts!"

"No, I wouldn't," Potts agreed, eyeing him suspiciously. "I never ask no questions. What do you boys want to know what Peter bought the blades for?"

"We want to hire him to do a job for us," Jim said, gravely. "Colonel Morrell is thinking of building a new school and he wants Peter to saw up the lumber for him!"

"For lands sake! You don't saw up lumber with a steel metal-cutting blade. Look here, are you boys poking fun at me?"

The boys looked from one to the other in silence and then Douglas shook his head. "It is horribly bad manners to poke at anyone, Mr. Potts. We wouldn't think of it. Well, thanks for your information. So long."

The cadets walked out of the local hardware store, leaving Mr. Potts in an uncertain frame of mind. He shook his head and went back to work, addressing his clerk briefly.

"Them cadets must be crazy. Such looney talk I never heard!"

On the way out to the unkempt street that had been named Meadow Street Don chuckled.

"Mr. Potts never asks questions, gentlemen! But he was just dying to know what we had in mind!"

"I'll say," laughed Hudson. "And if we had told him it would have spread all over town like wildfire."

There were only four or five houses on Meadow Street and they had no trouble in finding the one owned by the laborer Peter Cozoza. The man was not home and his small, undersized wife stared in awe at the six erect cadets who so completely blocked up her back door. She was somewhat charmed because they took off their military hats while they talked to her and they spoke gently and courteously, something with which Mrs. Cozoza was none too familiar. She told them, in answer to their inquiry, that her husband was not at home.

"Not at home, Mrs. Cozoza?" Jim replied, blankly. Douglas addressed the little woman next.

"Was he at home last Wednesday night?"

Don grasped his arm warningly. "I'm not altogether sure we ought to ask her that, Doug," he cautioned. "Might get her in trouble with the husband. You know how these people are."

But the little woman answered frankly enough. "No, mister, he go out last Wednesday night, I not know where. Since then he go down in the swamp a lot. You see, his boots muddy."

She pointed to a pair of muddy rubber boots that stood beside the stove. Jim quickly snapped up the lead offered.

"Down in the swamps?" he asked. "Which way? That

way?"

He pointed at random toward the black swamp that crept up close to the house, but Mrs. Cozoza shook her head. "No, down the path, there." She pointed to a path that showed faintly through the trees.

"Oh, I see," smiled Jim. "Well, that is all, thank you."

They left the woman standing in the doorway, frankly puzzled, and looked at the path that led into the swamp. Hudson looked at his watch.

"We've got time to follow the path a little way, at least," he announced. "The fact that the man goes into the swamp may not have any bearing on the thing at all, and then again, it may. I suppose you all think it worth looking into?"

They all agreed on that point and took the path into the swamp. When they had entered the dark, rank woods they were compelled to spread out in single file and keep to the path, which in some places was little more than a mere ribbon. A false step would have meant a wet and muddy foot. Thick bushes grew close to the path and brushed against their coats as they made their way into the damp swamp.

"This is a first class swamp, by golly," commented Vench. "That guy must have something good in here to make him want to dive into a place like this very often."

After they had followed the path for at least a quarter of a mile, they came to a kind of island in the midst of the swamp mud. The ground here was a little harder than the rest, although it did not take a very determined kick to drive a heel down into soft black soil. They spread out on this island and beyond a clump of bushes they came upon a ramshackle hut.

"Hooray, there is the castle before us!" cried Terry.

"A hobo's castle, by the looks of it," Don said, as they approached it. "Hope there's nobody here now."

The hut was not large and appeared to be about the size of a one-car garage. A door, which was closed, faced them, and one window was in the place, a glassless window that stared at them like a vacant eye. Hudson thrust his head cautiously in this opening.

"Only empty space greets us," he said.

"Nothing in there at all?" Douglas asked.

Vench went around and opened the door. "Looks like a couple of bags of potatoes in one corner," he called.

They thronged in the narrow door and Don poked one shoe

against the bags in the corner. Then, as a look of understanding passed over his face, he turned swiftly to the others.

"Here are the eagles!" he cried.

"I thought as much," whooped Hudson, tearing at the mouth of the bag nearest him. "Sure enough, here they are."

They swiftly tore the sacking away and the brass eagles were disclosed, swathed in straw. A thorough examination showed that they had not been damaged.

"So here is where they were taken," murmured Vench, looking around the hut.

"Yes, and who would ever think of looking for them out here?" put in Douglas. "If it hadn't been for Jim's chance discovery we would never have thought to look here."

"Things worked out in great shape all around," Jim said. "Well, now that we have the big birds, what—"

"Look!" cried Don, suddenly. "Here come some men!"

Chapter 12
The Eagles Are Rescued

Looking out of the window of the hut the cadets saw three men coming down the swamp pathway toward the hut. They were apparently laborers. Two of them were big men, the third was short but sufficiently heavy to be formidable. A single look convinced the boys that the men were coming toward them for no good purpose.

"I'll bet those characters mean to take our eagles away from us," Vench said in a low voice.

Hudson clenched his fists. "If they do, they'll be up against one of the finest fights of their lives," he promised, his jaw set determinedly. "We're not going to give up the eagles now that we have them in our hands."

"That's right," Don backed him up. "We'll put up a fight. Suppose we spring a surprise on them?"

"How do you mean, spring it?" Terry asked.

"Suppose only three of us go out and start walking away with the eagles? Then, if they mean to fight, they'll charge three of us, and the others can charge them from the rear. What do you say to that?"

"It's a good idea," Hudson said, briskly. "Don, Terry and I will go first, while Doug, Vench and Jim wait, ready to turn the tide if they should attack us. Are we all ready? Let's go."

Carrying the eagles between them Don, Hudson and Terry left the hut in the swamp and began to cross the open space before the shack. The three cadets in reserve watched them from their post and waited. When the three men saw the cadets coming they halted.

"Hey, where you go?" the short man called out, scowling sullenly.

"We're going back to school with these eagles," Hudson replied, his heart beating a trifle more rapidly than usual. "Then we're going to see to it that the fellows who stole the eagles go to jail for it!"

A frightened look passed between the men and the short man whispered something to his companions. One of the taller men growled loudly.

"They're only chucking a bluff. I'm for beatin' them up and pitchin' the eagles into the swamp. That's to teach them soldier boys to mind their own business!"

"I guess it is pretty much our business when you come and steal our ornaments off of the front steps!" growled Terry, his cheeks showing a red that did not appear there very often. "You big overgrown bullies get out of the way or we'll put you in the mud instead of the eagles!"

The big man pushed up his sleeves and advanced threateningly. "Let's spread a little o' this nice black mud on these kids," he invited. "It'll take some of the freshness out of them."

Seeing that they meant business, the cadets dropped the eagles and waited on the defensive.

Hudson deliberately picked out the biggest man and drove at him, avoiding his grasping hands and planting a light tap on his chest. Terry was exchanging lively blows with the other big man and the little man ran at Don. He did not seem to be as determined about it as the other two did, and Don, noting the fact, decided to finish him off rapidly. He ducked under the outflung arm of the short man, allowed him to flop half across his back, and then, with a well-timed heave, sent him flying over his back, to land heavily in the mud. Before he could get up Don leaped on him and a vigorous threshing battle ensued.

The two big men were more than a match for Terry and Hudson and they were out to deliberately break bones and hurt as viciously as possible. Under any other circumstances the reserve cadets would have held in for a time, but realizing the character of the men who were opposing their friends the three cadets rushed out of the hut and threw themselves on the men. Vench made a flying tackle at the man who was trying to crush Terry in his arms and Douglas and Jim rushed Hudson's foe. Before this onrush the men went down in the mud.

"The whole confounded school is here!" yelled the leader as he went down.

"Speaking of dipping us in the mud," panted Hudson. "Try it yourself!" And he deliberately pushed the head of the man so that his nose burrowed into the soft soil.

Realizing that they were in a bad position the two big men exerted all their strength in the struggle and finally broke away from the lighter cadets. They wasted no time but fled down the path, leaving the boys winded and bruised, for the fight, though short, had been determined. Vench was for chasing them, but Hudson was against it.

"Nothing doing," he cried. "Those men know the path and we don't. Don's still got his man."

The short laborer had made a strong effort to get away from Don, but the cadet had held onto him grimly, knocking him down with each attempt to get up. The others went to his aid and they hauled both Don and the man to their feet. The man gave one despairing look around and then, realizing that he was trapped, whimpered brokenly.

"Please! No send Peter to jail! Peter not a bad man! I not mean to hurt you!"

"Are you Peter Cozoza?" asked Don, wiping the mud from his face and his overcoat.

The man nodded miserably. "Oh, please, not de jail. Think, mister, Maretta and de five keeds! What dey do if Peter in jail?"

"You won't go to jail," Douglas reassured him. "All we want you to do is to talk. Did you saw the eagles off up at the school?"

The man nodded. "I was paid to do it, mister! Peter not a bad man, but he need de money so bad!"

The cadets understood readily. "Sure, we know that, Peter," Don said. "You were paid to cut them off. Who paid you to go up to our school and cut off the eagles?"

The man hesitated, but feeling that the truth would serve him better than a lie, spoke out. "A man name Mr. Gates, up at the big house, he tell me!"

"Sure!" nodded Jim, grimly. "Of course, it would be Mr. Gates."

"But why?" asked Vench.

"Oh, just to make us feel that he was right about his stand against Dimsdale," Don answered, wearily. "Just a petty, baby-ish revenge, that is all. He got these three men to take away the eagles so that it would cast reflections on Dimsdale. Maybe he even hoped to plant the eagles on their property later on, I don't know. Or, if they were never found he would allow the suspicion between the two schools to rankle for years to come. You can't say anything bad enough about a man like that."

"You bet you can't," agreed the captain. "How did you know we were down here, Peter?"

"My wife, she tell me when I stop up there with my two

friends," the laborer replied.

"You just listen here, Peter," Terry lectured. "In the future you stop having such kind of friends, do you hear? We're going to be good to you and not take you to jail, just because we wouldn't want to be mean to your wife and the kids, see? But if we ever catch you hanging around with bad men like that again, we'll see that you go away to the big prison for years and years. See, Mr. Peter?"

"Yes, yes!" the man agreed, eagerly. "I will make good friends always, like you!"

"Thanks for the compliment!" laughed Hudson. "Now, we'd better get out of here. Peter, you show us the way down the path, and no funny business!"

They picked up the brass eagles, which were quite heavy, and following Peter, lugged them down the path. It was growing dark and it seemed a long way back, but in time they stood in the back yard of the Cozoza house.

"Another thing, Peter," Don said to the laborer, as they prepared to set out for the village. "We want you to keep quiet about the whole thing. If you don't, we'll have to go back on our promise about the jail. If Mr. Gates should ask you about the eagles you tell him some of the soldier boys came and took them away, and that you couldn't stop them. Outside of that we want you to keep your mouth closed about the whole business. Understand?"

"Yes, sir. I keep ver' quiet!" the man promised.

They left him and trudged down to the village. The eagles were getting heavier all the time and Jim proposed that they hire a cab to take them up to the school.

"Good idea," approved Douglas. "These things get heavier with every step. I guess we can scare up a dollar or two between us, can't we?"

They found that between them they had a few dollars and they hailed a passing cab. Gratefully they piled in and told the driver to take them to Woodcrest.

"What you got in them bags, boys?" the driver, a town character, said as they drove up the hill toward the school.

"Flower pots!" returned Terry, promptly.

"You don't say!" cried the driver, sending out a cloud of smoke from his battered pipe. "Must have quite a number of pots in those bags!"

"Oh, we have," Terry returned. "You see, the colonel is

thinking of relandscaping the whole school, so we're going to put plenty of flowers around."

Almost the first one that they met in the hall when they carried the rescued eagles into the school was the colonel himself.

"Where in the world have you been, boys?" the headmaster cried. "And where did you collect all that mud?"

"We've been putting in a strenuous afternoon getting back the eagles, sir!" replied the senior captain. "Here they are."

The story was swiftly told and then the cadets went upstairs to clean up. Like wildfire the story ran around the building and the six boys were admired by the others for their work.

It was decided to send a public apology to Dimsdale for holding that school in suspicion, and this was done and graciously accepted. Then Dimsdale acted by having a scorching editorial printed in the town paper in answer to the one suggested by Melvin Gates. The conduct of his son years ago was broadly hinted at and the good name of the Gates family was crushed once and for all in that locality.

"Do you think that will drive them out of the town?" Don and Jim asked the colonel, as they were discussing the editorial with him.

"I don't know," the colonel replied, slowly. "I hardly think so, for they only recently bought the house they are living in and that may be a big factor in keeping them here. I hope they do stay, for I'm still hopeful that we'll find out why young Gates took that cup. Of course, this editorial practically ruins the family with decent people, but the Gates' have money enough to keep to themselves and pass it off."

"You yourself did not say anything to Melvin Gates, did you?" Don asked.

"No, that wasn't necessary. As you saw for yourselves, the Dimsdale editorial was a scorcher and that was enough. Gates' trick was simply an attempt at petty revenge that backfired. We'll just have our eagles remounted and forget all about the whole thing."

"OK," nodded Jim. "Now that the Gates family is well established in Portville, perhaps we can learn something important about that cup business."

Chapter 13
The Call for Help

Mr. Terry Mackson chuckled and looked over the edge of his blanket at the other two beds in the room. In the farthest bed Jim Mercer was sleeping with just a bit of noise proceeding from his throat. On the bed near Terry, Don slept in silence, his face turned toward the red-headed boy. Terry glanced back at the window and then put one bare foot out of bed.

It was the morning of the second Saturday in December and the weather man had sprung a surprise on the cadets. When they had gone to bed on the previous night it had been cold and clear, but during the night the weather had magically changed. Terry, lightest sleeper of the three friends, had awakened early, to find the world wrapped in a whirling, blowing snowstorm, the soft white flakes banked in little piles against their windows.

For a single moment Terry had lain there contemplating the beauty of the early morning scene and then the light of mischief had dawned in his gray eyes. Consulting his watch he perceived that it was almost time for the bugle to blow, so he had no compunctions about what he intended to do. With the grace of a stalking cat the red-head crept to the window and scooped in a handful of snow. Keeping a wary eye on the two sleepers he made himself about five small sized snowballs and placed them on his bed. Then he dipped his hands once more into the wet snow and gathered a large quantity.

Making his way with extreme caution he reached Jim's bed and gently pulled the covers off that young man's feet. Against the warm feet of the boy he placed the snow, and then, bounding over to Don, he placed a small pile on his forehead. From there it was but a single bound into bed, where he pulled up the covers over his chin, and carefully hiding the snowballs, pretended to sleep.

It was not a moment too soon. Jim sat up suddenly, drawing his feet in a convulsive movement toward him. A running trickle of cold water woke Don at the same time.

"Hey, who piled snow against my feet?" demanded Jim,

knocking the cold stuff onto the floor with a single sweep.

"Probably the same one who put a mound of it on my head," retorted Don, and the two brothers looked suspiciously at Terry.

But this aspect baffled them for a moment. Apparently, the red-head was fast asleep. Only a very little part of him showed above his cover, and a gentle sound, indicating deep breathing, came from the bed. But the more the brothers looked, the more suspicious they became.

"That looks too innocent to suit me," Jim announced, and began to get out of bed.

"Yes, I doubt that peaceful, dreamy look on his homely face," chimed in Don, throwing off his covers.

The boy in bed stirred and apparently woke up, flashing them a happy smile. "Good morning, Don; good morning, Jim," he greeted, quietly. Then he sat up and looked with wondering astonishment out of the window. "Why bless my soul, it has snowed, hasn't it?"

"Yes," replied Jim, coming nearer. "And let me tell you, Chucklehead, that it has been a remarkable storm. It snowed right in under my covers and piled up against my feet, and there was even a little mound on my brother's head!"

"No!" cried the red-headed boy, in astonishment.

"Yes," cried Jim. "And now we're going to hang you out the window to get a little snow on you!"

"No, you're not!" retorted Terry, bringing five melting snowballs into sudden view. "Here is where the artillery goes into action!"

Five snowballs sped in rapid succession across the room, three of them landing on Jim and Don. They managed to dodge the other two, and then, seeing that his ammunition was exhausted, they helped themselves to some snow from the window sill and faced him. Terry quickly raised a wall of bed covers before him.

"Don't bother to make snowballs," Jim begged. "I think we ought to do something useful with the snow. That lad's face is dirty!"

"I see what you mean," Don nodded. "It is kind of red. Too much of that red thatch on top of his head, and the color runs down on his face. Think we ought to wash it off?"

"Yep! Let's get busy," said Jim, earnestly.

"You keep away from me with that stuff!" grunted the boy,

as they hurled themselves on him. But the two brothers tore down his cover wall and proceeded to wash his freckled face vigorously, not without damage to themselves and their pajamas, for Terry fought like a wildcat. In the midst of the melee the bugle rang out.

Abandoning their fun the boys began to dress rapidly, chattering away about the welcome snow. It promised them a variety of sport, in the nature of snow battles and sledding, and they were eager to get out and into it.

"Luckily, it is only a half day," whooped Don, slipping into his coat. "We can get out into the snow soon after dinner. It's coming down steadily."

When they got downstairs they found only a few cadets ahead of them. Hudson was one of them. He stood out on the front steps, admiring the view across the rolling fields and hills. His back was toward the boys and Don quietly packed a snowball and threw it at him. It hit the senior captain on the back of the neck and he whirled around, grinning, intending to say something.

But he closed his mouth with a snap and waited. Just above Don's head was a tiny shed roof, and Hudson saw what was going to happen. A puffy drift had gathered there and a fierce swirl of wind hit it at the precise moment that he turned around. Hudson grinned broadly as the miniature snowslide hit Don on the shoulders, knocking off his hat and sifting in powdery masses down his neck. Don coughed and sputtered in surprise.

"Very neatly and efficiently done," cried Hudson lifting his hat politely to the snow drift. "I thank you!"

All through the morning classes the cadets were impatient and when the noon meal was over they piled out into the snow with zest and a sense of pleasure. By this time it had stopped snowing, leaving about a foot of snow carpeting the ground. The sun came out briefly and the cadets were alarmed lest it do some damage, but in the long run it turned out to be their friend. It melted enough of the white material to make it watery and then the cold air promptly froze it, making a delightful surface for coasting.

"Tonight we can go coasting on Nelson Hill!" cried Lieutenant Thompson.

Nelson Hill was a long stretch of sloping hillside less than a half mile west of the school, and the majority of the cadets were preparing to spend the evening with their sleds. Most of them had already started for the hill with barrel staves and miscellaneous wood, with which to build fires on top of the long slope. When Terry, Don, Jim and Vench stood around considering, the distressing fact was brought home to them that they had no sled.

"The seniors have got sleds," remarked Vench. "And so have the second class men. I guess that the newer men are out of luck."

Douglas approached them, excitement showing in his hurry. "You guys got a sled?" he hailed.

"No," replied Jim. "Have you?"

"I know where there is one!" was the satisfying reply. "There is an old bob-sled down in the boathouse, with a broken runner, that we can fix up. What do you say?"

"Is the iron runner broken?" Don asked quickly.

"No, but a wooden support is. The iron on it is all right, outside of being a bit rusty. Suppose we fix it up?"

The cadets needed no further invitation but rushed to the boathouse without delay, there to find the old bob-sled of which Douglas had spoken. The broken wooden support, running from the body of the sled to the iron runner, was not a serious problem, and between them they soon managed to get it out and substitute another one for it.

"There!" cried Jim, proudly. "As good as new, by golly!"

"Well, just about," agreed Vench. "If it was new it would have a little less dust on it, but as an A number one sled it is OK."

"We'll soon clean the dust off it," decided Douglas, and they got some water from the gym, a brush and soap, and went to work with a will, with the result that the sled was soon in a different condition.

"Too late to try her out before supper," decided Don, glancing out at the gathering darkness. "But we'll go over to the hill after we eat."

As soon as the evening meal was over Woodcrest Military school was nearly deserted, almost all of the cadets going toward the distant hill. Only a few boys, more interested in warm quarters and books, remained in the school to miss the fun.

The friends ran down to the boathouse, uncovered the bob, which they had hidden under some loose canvas, and placing it on the snow, pulled it at a rapid pace toward Nelson Hill. It took them a good half hour to get there, as it was uphill most of the way. The cadets who had arrived before them had lighted fires, which blazed against the black sky like flaming beacons, and by the light of these fires the cadets were coasting. The hill was long and sloping and gave them a good ride, and by the same token, a good stiff walk up again.

The hill was covered with sleds. Shouts of laughter and merry yells echoed and re-echoed over the surrounding country as the cadets enjoyed the fun. Generosity prevailed, the cadets loaning their sleds to those who had none, while the lenders warmed themselves around the fires and waited for the borrowers to toil up the hill again.

"Well, what say to our first trip down?" called Douglas, planting the bob firmly on the brow of the hill.

"OK," agreed Vench, sitting on the sled. Douglas eyed him with vast disapproval.

"What are you going to do, sit on the sled?" he demanded.

"Certainly," retorted Vench. "What am I supposed to do, stand on it?"

"You ought to know enough about tobogganing to lie down," Douglas said. "Only girls sit up. Do you want me to clasp my hands around your tummy and scream when we hit a bump?"

"Aw, go chase yourself!" growled Vench, lying down on the front of the sled. Jim and Terry followed and Don squirmed on top of them. There was now just room enough for Douglas.

"All set?" inquired Douglas, taking hold of the rear of the sled.

"Let her go!" the others cried, and Douglas gave the bob a push. It began to tilt over the top of the hill and moved slowly down. Douglas sprang on, kneeling on the little space left for him, and the bob, with its heavy load, began to move with increasing speed down the hill. It did not immediately gain a great rate of speed for the runners were still a little rusty, but it picked up gradually, until it was fairly flying down the hill.

Past single sleds they went, Vench steering dexterously in and out between them, passing cadets toiling up the snowy slopes, who turned to stare after them. One or two light bumps were encountered, which caused the sled to jump a few inches from the ground, and they literally flew through the air, to land with a jarring thud a little further on. In this way they reached the bottom of the hill and kept going on the level ground, to stop finally a long way from the point at which they had started.

"That was great!" cried Don, springing up.

"The fires look to be a long way up in the air," observed Vench, and they looked up to the top of the hill.

The fires looked far away from where they were, sending licking yellow flames against a deep black sky. A number of black dots were streaking down the hill in their direction, but the bob had gone further than any of them because of its weight.

"Now I suppose we have got to walk up again," said Terry. "Too bad we can't push a button and make the hill reverse for us!"

"Why go up right away?" asked Jim. "Here is a smaller hill. Want to try it?"

A few yards from them a smaller slope showed, on which the hard snow gleamed from the faraway fires.

"We'll run right down into the woods, if we go down this hill," cautioned Don. "However, I'm perfectly willing. Want to try it?"

The others agreed and with another push they dipped down this second hill, taking a long ride in between the trees that closed over their heads and shut out all light. But when they came to compare notes they found that sentiment was not very keen for this hill.

"Nothing to it," declared Vench.

"The snow is packed harder on the long hill," Jim decided. "No use using these little ones when we have a perfectly good big one."

"No," agreed Douglas, gathering up the rope of the bob-sled. "Well, we might as well begin our upward hike."

"Wait a minute!" cried Don. "Did you hear a crash just then?"

None of them had. "Must have been some snow falling, or an old tree crashing down," Terry suggested. They turned to go back but once more Don stopped them.

"Listen!" he cried. "Someone's calling!"

They stopped and were silent for a long interval, but there was no sound. Vench laughed.

"Don's hearing things," he said. "We'll have to get him back to the top of the hill right away."

"No, I tell you I did hear something," insisted Don. "Listen, there it is again!"

This time, clearly and distinctly on the night air, a call echoed through the woods.

"Help!" cried a faint muffled voice. "Help, somebody!"

Chapter 14
Inside Gates' House

"Someone is in trouble!" cried Vench, as the startled cadets looked at each other in the dense gloom.

"Yes, and we had better get on the job," announced Don, with decision. "The call came from over this way."

"Shall we leave the bob here?" Douglas asked.

"Might as well," Jim nodded. "It will only be in the way. We can easily find it when we come back."

There was no sound from the one who had called out a few moments ago, but the boys had the direction in mind, so they struck off into the tangle of the woods without further delay. They had gone about two hundred yards when they came upon a country road which had been cut through the woods.

"I wonder if the call came from this road?" mused Don, as they halted in perplexity.

"I think it did," Terry replied. "I don't believe that it was in the woods. Shall we split into two parties?"

"You mean one go up and one down the road?" Don asked.

"Yes. You and I will go east and Vench, Doug and Jim can go west. We'll sing out if we see anything."

This plan was agreed to and the boys set out, Terry and Don running along the road in the general direction of Portville. But they had not gone far before someone whistled back of them.

"That's Jim," Don said, as they halted. "They must have found something. Let's go back."

Accordingly, they turned around and ran back, passing the spot where they had split and continuing on until they came to a bend in the snow-covered road. Around this bend they found the other boys gathered around a small automobile, the nose of which was smashed against a tree. The three boys were busy around the car as Don and Terry hastened up. By the faint light of the one headlight that was burning the two boys could see that a figure was hunched over the wheel of the club coupe. The others were trying to pull the man out and finding it a trying task, for the driver was tightly pinned by the wheel, which had rammed into his stomach.

"His feet are free," announced Douglas, who had been giving his attention to them. Don grasped the bent steering wheel and exerted all of his strength. It yielded a little and he tugged some more.

"Pull, you guys," he commanded, and they drew the body of the driver from the car. The man was unconscious and groaned slightly. When they had placed him on the snow in the road they saw that it was Melvin Gates.

"Somebody run and get the bob-sled," directed Don, and Vench and Douglas dashed into the woods at once. Quickly and efficiently Don ran his hands over the man's arms and legs.

"No bones broken that I can feel," he announced. "However, he may be internally injured, and it is possible that some of his ribs are broken. I wonder if we ought to move him?"

"We've got to," decided Terry as the others appeared with the big sled. "He must be taken home or to a doctor's at once. We'll lift him gently onto the sled and get going right away."

There was a blanket in the car and this they spread on the sled. Then, with infinite care they placed the limp body of the elder Gates on the sled and covered him up protectingly. Don and Douglas took the rope and began to pull the sled, while Terry, Jim and Vench brought up the rear and helped by pushing.

"Don't you thing somebody had better run ahead and get a doctor?" asked Vench.

"Yes," nodded Don. "We're not far from Portville, and we'll take Gates right to his home. Suppose you and Jim run ahead and get a doctor, and we'll take Mr. Gates to his own house."

"OK," cried Jim, and he and Vench set off at a brisk trot and soon were lost to sight down the winding road.

"Car must have skidded on the road," observed Douglas, as they pulled the sled with its silent burden.

"It did," agreed Don. "I noticed the marks on the snow. This old road must be a shortcut to Portville and Mr. Gates was taking it on the way home from wherever he has been. The snow just at that point was pretty hard and slippery and the car hit the tree, buckling up. That was the crash that I heard."

"It must have been," Douglas replied. "Do you think he'll die?"

"Hard to tell," shrugged Don. "We can't be sure how badly

he is hurt inside. I hope we aren't far from Portville."

They were not, but it seemed like a longer journey than it actually was. Terry helped greatly by pushing and guiding the sled over obstructions and places that would have jarred the man. Now and then they heard low groans from Mr. Gates, but he did not regain consciousness.

Don knew the Gates' home by a description which the colonel had given him and they had no difficulty in finding it. Since there was no hospital nearby they knew that their best plan was to get Gates to his own home as soon as possible. It was with a vast sense of relief that they ran the bob-sled up the driveway of the Gates home and came to a halt before the wide front doors.

"Well, I'm glad that is over!" murmured Terry, straightening his aching back.

Don ran swiftly up the front porch and rang the bell madly. It seemed an unusually long time before a very deliberate and correct butler opened the door. He stared at Don with expressionless eyes.

"Mr. Gates has been hurt," Don cried. "Get his bed ready and open these doors wide, so that we can carry him upstairs."

The butler came to life, his correctness vanished and he ran with undignified but practical haste up the front stairs, calling aloud for the younger Mr. Gates. Don opened the front doors as wide as they would go just as Arthur Gates and his wife appeared anxiously in the doorway. Without paying any attention to their frightened inquiries Don ran back to Douglas and Terry.

"Lift him gently," Don said, and the three boys exerted all their care as they raised the elder Gates from the sled. At that same moment a car stopped at the front gate and the doctor, with Jim and Vench, jumped from the car. Arthur Gates lent a helping hand to the cadets and together they carried the old man up the front stairs and to his luxurious bedroom on the second floor. When they had laid him on the bed the boys quietly withdrew, leaving Gates, his wife and the doctor alone in the room with the injured man, while the agitated butler patrolled the upper hall.

"Do you suppose we had better beat it?" Douglas whispered, after Don had closed the front doors and kicked some loose snow outside.

"No, we'll stay and see if his condition is serious," Don

replied.

"But his family is none too friendly with us," Douglas persisted.

"I guess all that will be forgotten in a time like this," Don answered.

The cadets waited. The house had become quiet after the first flurry of excitement and no one appeared to be downstairs. To Don this state of affairs was gratifying, for he had a plan in mind. Taking care not to seem too curious he edged away from the others, who were looking at some magazines on the table, and in time made his way around the downstairs floor on a tour of inspection, keeping a wary eye about for a possible maid or the upset butler.

He looked into a large room off the library in which the cadets were gathered and found that it was the dining room. From there he moved to the door which opened into a large living room, and he looked carefully at every object on the mantelpiece. There was a small study near that which he looked over, and then the hall and library. He returned to the others when his tour of inspection was over.

"The cup is not downstairs," he reflected. "I didn't think it would be in plain sight anywhere, but I wanted to make sure."

After a considerable delay Arthur Gates came down the central stairs and joined them. His face was pale and he showed signs of anxiety, but his message was a cheering one.

"Nothing really serious," he told them, in answer to their eager question. "There are no bones broken and outside of a bad bruising my father is all right. It was a narrow escape, however. Tell me how you found him and how you happened to get a doctor here so quickly."

The boys told him and Gates was impressed. "It was very lucky for all concerned that you happened to be at that particular point in the woods," he said. "My father had been over to Easton and was taking the old road home again. If he had remained there the result would have been far different. I don't know how to express my appreciation to you."

"Don't try," begged Don. "We were just lucky enough to be there at the time. We are glad to hear that your father is not in any danger."

Gates' eyes wandered to their uniforms. "You are cadets up at Woodcrest, aren't you?"

"Yes," the boys nodded. Gates was silent for a moment. "I

shall see to it that Colonel Morrell knows of your service to us."

"Don't bother," said Don, glancing at the clock. "We are late now and we'll have to report our reason for staying over the limit, so the colonel will find it out from us. That will be sufficient. When you come right down to it, it didn't amount to much on our part."

"You fellows are too modest," smiled Gates, as he saw them out.

They retrieved the bob-sled and started back for the school at a rapid pace. Terry whistled as they walked along.

"Well, it was quite a night," he observed. "I'm glad the old gentleman wasn't hurt badly."

"So am I," agreed Don. "But it all served one useful purpose. We know where the Gates home is and I know what the inside of it looks like. Don't know if that will ever do us any good or not, but it may come in handy some day."

Chapter 15
Arthur Gates' Letter

The following day Don decided to walk to town and see if there was a letter for him at the postoffice. He expected one from his father. The others were studying so Don went alone to the town. He could have waited until the mail was delivered to the school, but that would be over the weekend, and he did not feel like waiting. He walked to town and entered the local postoffice.

A number of persons were waiting for their mail, so he took his place in line and waited patiently. A man ahead of him looked familiar to Don, and when the man had obtained his mail he turned away from the window and Don saw that it was Arthur Gates.

Gates had a number of letters in his hand, some of which he had received at the window and some of which he intended to mail. He passed Don and the boy paid no further attention to him. Don got his letter and left the window. As he did so he saw Gates walk to the door, open it, and as he was going out, drop a letter.

Don stepped forward and picked up the letter which Gates had dropped. The man was evidently in a hurry, for he passed out of the door and walked down the street rapidly. Thinking that the letter was one which Gates had intended to mail Don decided to drop it in the slot himself, but when he got to the mail opening he noted that the letter was addressed to Gates, and that it was postmarked Canada.

"Shucks," he muttered in disgust. "Now I've got to go and catch him."

With this thought in mind Don darted out of the door and looked down the darkened street for Gates, but he was not to be seen. He walked to the corner and looked up and down but without success. Gates was nowhere in sight. Feeling that he must go back and leave the letter with the postmaster Don was on the point of returning when a church clock struck the hour.

"Golly," he reflected. "I haven't time. I'll have to get back to school at once, and on the double."

There was no time to drop the letter off at Gates' house and Don decided to put it in his pocket and take it around to the house on the following day when he took his regular Sunday afternoon walk. He thrust it deep into his pocket and half walking, half running, reached the school building just in time. Without even thinking of the letter which did not belong to him he hung up his overcoat and went to supper.

It was not until after supper that he again thought of the letter and then he went to the room. Jim and Terry were in the Recreation Hall, watching a game of chess between two upper classmen, and Don was alone in the room. He took the letter from his pocket, stared at it, thrust his hand quickly into the pocket and then uttered a cry of dismay.

"Wet!" he cried. "I must have gotten some snow in my pocket and it has soaked the letter through. Darn it, the glue on the envelope has come off."

The envelope had indeed opened and the letter was wet through on one end. He decided to dry the paper and without any intention of looking at its contents pulled the dampened sheets out of the bedraggled envelope and spread them on top of the table.

"There, that will dry in a short time," he thought. "Then I'll seal it up and explain about it to Mr. Gates tomorrow."

The last sheet was turned up toward him. He glanced at it and was about to turn away, when a word struck his attention. He looked down and then hesitated.

"Humph, I musn't read this," he thought. "I shouldn't even have it. But—"

Then he decided to see what the word "cup" was about. He picked up the letter and read the paragraph. It read as follows:

"I understand your anxiety about that trophy cup that has caused all of the trouble, and I will do my best to help you. As long as I and George Long are the only ones who know the full story about that cup, I feel it my duty to help you in any way that I can. I was wondering why you didn't take the thing to a jeweler and have the bottom scraped, but I can see what that would have meant, and the best thing is to get it away from your house. There is no telling who might some day get ahold of the thing and find out the truth, and with those cadets in the same town such a thing wouldn't be wise. I will be down to see you in a week's time, and when I return to Canada I'll take the cup with me and will keep it safely in my cabin here. When you come to visit me next summer we can scrape the bottom ourselves or we can throw it in the river, whatever you say. Too bad you ever did such an outlandish thing."

The letter was signed "Oliver Burgess."

"Now, what the devil can that mean?" puzzled the astonished Don. "It is surely referring to the missing 1933 trophy, but I wonder what all that stuff about the scraping of the bottom means?"

Chapter 16
News from Inside

"So he is worrying about the cup, eh?" asked the colonel, when Don and Jim showed him the strange letter.

At the colonel's suggestion they had read the entire thing, taking the responsibility upon themselves in view of the fact that every effort to clear George Long was justifiable. But outside of the one passage that Don had read there was no other clue in the letter.

"He seems to be," Don answered. "What do you make of that part about scraping the bottom of the cup, sir?"

"I don't know what to make of it," the headmaster confessed. "It is very strange, and I'm afraid that we will have to get possession of the cup in order to find out just what all this mystery is. We must get the cup."

"If we do get it, we'll have to work fast," Jim put in. "This friend of his is to take it away to Canada with him."

"Yes," agreed the colonel. "We will have to work fast. In the meantime, I shall have a copy of this letter made and then we'll seal it up and one of you should take it to the postoffice and drop it in the incoming mail slot. In that way Gates will get it without ever knowing that it had been tampered with."

The colonel had a copy made of the letter and then Don and Jim walked down to the postoffice and placed it in the proper slot.

In a day or two the colonel reported very satisfactory developments. He showed Don an advertisement in the town paper. The advertisement read as follows:

"Wanted: A butler for large household, must have previous experience and good references. Apply at any hour to 14 Portville Avenue and ask for Mr. Melvin Gates."

"That ad just suits our purpose and couldn't be better," the colonel told Don.

"How so, sir?" asked Don, puzzled.

The colonel laughed. "I'll show you this afternoon. Go to Captain Rhodes and tell him I have excused you from drill formation, then come and report to me. We will take a little drive together."

After classes that day Don reported to Rhodes and repeated the colonel's order, and the drill instructor readily excused him from duty. While the other cadets were drilling on the windswept field Don went to the colonel's office to accompany the headmaster on his unknown journey. The colonel was ready for him and when Don entered he called up a local taxi agency and ordered a cab.

"We are going in style—and in secrecy," the colonel chuckled, amused at the wondering look on the cadet's face.

In due time the taxi arrived and the colonel and Don got into the cab, after the headmaster had given an order to the driver in a low tone. When they were safely underway Colonel Morrell told Don that they were going to call on the police.

"A sort of a diplomatic excursion," he smiled. "The fewer who see us, the better."

They rode down into Portville and stopped at last in front of the town hall, where the colonel alighted, paid his bill and then led Don inside and into a small private office, where they remained alone for some fifteen minutes. At last a small door opened and Captain Dorran of the local police came into the room. He was an old friend of the colonel's and they shook hands heartily.

"This is one of my cadets, cap'n," remarked the colonel, nodding to Don. "One of my very best, too, the young man who helped me out of that bad scrape last year."

"Glad to know you, young man," the police chief laughed. "I thought at first that the colonel was bringing you to me for business purposes!"

"We have some business on hand," said the colonel, as Don shook hands with the police chief. "And we'll want a little help from you."

"Sit down, both of you," Dorran invited. "Now what can I do to help you?"

"Don," directed the colonel, "tell Captain Dorran the whole class trophy story up to date. Don't leave a thing out."

Don complied, being careful to remember and relate everything that had happened, and when he had finished the colonel nodded in approval.

"Yes, that is about right. What do you think of it, Dorran?"

The chief frowned. "This Arthur Gates is a pretty black character, isn't he? What is it that you want me to do, Morrell?"

"There was an advertisement in the paper last night calling for a butler, and the Gates family placed the ad. I want you to scare me up a good detective that will pass as a butler, and have him placed in the house. When the man from Canada comes this butler-detective is to try and get hold of that cup, or at least to prevent it from going to Canada. Can you do that?"

"I think I can," replied the chief promptly. "I'll have Proctor come in."

Mr. Proctor was called in and the colonel and Don saw he could play the part well. He looked anything but a detective, with his expressionless face, soft brown eyes and sleek hair. He did look every inch a soft-spoken, efficient butler. He was informed of the necessary details and ordered to either get the cup or at least keep it from going to Canada. Even before Don and the colonel left the station he was on his way to Gates' place to apply, with references in his pocket that had served him more than once in similar cases.

"Well, what do you think of my plan?" the colonel asked his young companion on the way back to school in the cab.

"I think it should be just the thing to clear up all this business," Don replied. "We know that the cup is in the house and the detective should be able to get hold of it. Once we get a good look at the thing we should be able to clear up all the mystery surrounding it and then George Long can be wholly cleared."

"Yes, that's what I think," Colonel Morrell nodded. "When I do announce the story of George's innocence to the world I don't want any loose ends. I want to be able to tell the whole story. I think the detective is clever enough to get the cup and then we'll be at the end of our problem."

Some of the cadets were standing around the door when the cab stopped and they were surprised to see Don alight and hold the door open for the colonel, who got out and paid the driver. The colonel went on inside and Don lingered to talk to some of his friends. He came in for a lot of good-natured bantering for going riding with the colonel.

"It beats me," said Lieutenant Thompson, with mock seriousness, "how some fellows do get along in this world. Here the rest of us go out and drill all afternoon, while Don goes riding in a taxi with the colonel! Some fellows have all the luck!"

The colonel kept Don fully informed of the progress of

events at the Gates home. Mr. Proctor had become butler at the house and in two days' time reported the arrival of the friend from Canada. As yet the detective had not been able to find the missing trophy, but he believed that it would soon be forthcoming.

The next report came in one evening while Don and Jim were making out a report in the colonel's office. The telephone rang out and the colonel answered it. They heard him say: "What? That's fine. Get hold of it in some way, and bring it right up to the school when you do. That's good news. All right, and best of luck."

He turned to the boys and lowered his voice. "That was Mr. Proctor," he told them. "The friend from Canada is going home tomorrow, and in addition to his regular suitcase, which he brought with him, he is carrying a small black bag, and if he does not get an opportunity to get the bag in the house, he will follow the man to the railroad station and try to get it there. He'll get it somehow, and I told him to bring it right up here to the school when he did get it."

"That is good news from inside," said Don, with satisfaction. "I hope he manages it."

Chapter 17
Mr. Proctor Gets the Bag

Saturday evening, the telephone in Colonel Morrell's office rang. After a short conversation he sent an orderly in quest of Don and Jim, as well as Douglas and Hudson. When they were all assembled he told them what he had in mind.

"I have just had a call from Mr. Proctor, boys. He has the black bag with the 1933 trophy in it!"

"He has?" cried Don. "That's fine."

"Yes, and he is on his way here now. I wanted you young men on the spot to get a good look at it as soon as I did. All we have to do is to wait until the detective comes."

It took Mr. Proctor a good half hour to arrive, but at last they heard a taxi drive up to the front of Locke Hall and a door slam. A moment later and Mr. Proctor was with them, a satisfied expression on his sleek face. In his hand he carried a small black bag, of which he took excellent care.

"Well, so we have it at last, eh?" boomed the colonel. "How did you get hold of it?"

"I didn't get it in the house at all," the detective explained. "Mr. Burgess, the visitor from Canada, kept it so close beside him that I didn't have a chance. I had to wait until after he was gone. I followed him down to the station and watched my chance, but it didn't come until after I got on the train. He had placed it in the rack overhead and when we came to a small station I got up, took the bag and made for the door, just as he raised a cry. It was good and dark, so I just beat it away and took a cab here. I called you up from Orangeville, colonel."

"I see," said the colonel. "Well, now let's have a look at that cup."

Mr. Proctor went to work on the bag, which was locked, but with the aid of some keys and a huge knife forced the top open, while the cadets looked on in breathless interest. As the bag split open with a rush they all craned forward to see what was in it.

It was full of old newspapers, and nothing more.

For just a minute there was complete silence in the room.

The boys looked from one to another and the detective looked as though his eyes would pop out with surprise and mortification. The colonel breathed hard.

"Looks as though something had been put over on you, Mr. Proctor," he said quietly.

The detective nodded miserably. All the way to the school he had been congratulating himself on his cleverness and now it turned out to be but a mockery.

"Then he must have the thing in his suitcase!" he cried. "But I distinctly heard Gates tell him to take the cup in the black bag."

"It looks very much as though they both knew you were on the trail and switched the cup to the suitcase," Hudson remarked.

"If that is the case, the cup is lost, for it is on its way to Canada," the colonel declared.

"I don't see how they could have gotten onto me," the detective cried. "I never did a better job in my life."

"I have just thought of something," ventured Don. "Do you remember the night you called up the school here and told the colonel all about it, Mr. Proctor?"

"Yes," replied the man.

"Was Arthur Gates at home when you called?"

"Yes, but he was upstairs, for I made sure of that. Oh, he couldn't have heard me!" the man protested.

"When I was at that house, on the night we took Mr. Gates home from the accident, I noticed a telephone upstairs. Do you suppose—"

"Ah!" almost shouted the detective. "That click on the wire!"

"Did it sound as though someone upstairs picked up the telephone receiver while you were talking?" pressed Don quietly.

"Yes," acknowledged the detective. "Now that you put it that way, it did. I remember hearing a click while I was explaining things to Colonel Morrell, but I thought nothing of it. Somebody, probably Arthur Gates himself, must have heard that conversation."

After the crestfallen detective had departed they talked it over, realizing that the game was up. There was now no hope of ever recovering the cup.

"I guess we'll just have to go without knowing what was

on that cup that made it worth while for Gates to steal," the colonel admitted. "Now, the only thing for me to do is to have another Alumni meeting soon after Christmas and have Long there. At that meeting we'll publicly clear him and let it go at that."

"All I can say is that Mr. Proctor is not the best detective in the world," said Douglas.

"No," seconded the colonel. "He should never have called up from the house, or from any other place. He should have come directly here and told me things personally. Well, boys, that is the end of the cup affair. I thank you most heartily for your very real interest in it and your services to Mr. Long. That ends the matter of the 1933 class's trophy as far as we are concerned, with the exception of the apology to Long."

Chapter 18
The Published List

Christmas came and Woodcrest was almost deserted. For a whole week the school looked empty and forlorn as the boys went to their homes to spend the holiday season.

The Mercers and Terry had returned to Maine, separating for a brief week to be with their own families. The Mercer brothers thoroughly enjoyed the week at home, visiting friends, spending time with the family, and getting in some fine skating.

It was the day following New Year's Day that the brothers returned to Woodcrest and once more plunged into the routine of school life. Things went along smoothly for a week, and then something unexpected happened.

Just as Don and Jim were cleaning up one evening for dinner Terry burst into the room, his eyes shining with excitement.

"A little excitement now and then, is relished by the best of men!" recited the red-headed boy.

"Admitting that I am the best of men, what is the excitement!" grinned Jim, carefully hanging up his towel.

"The Portville Bank was held up and robbed this afternoon!" came the startling answer.

"What's that?" Don exclaimed.

"Sure enough," affirmed Terry, bouncing down on the bed. "A big car drove up to the bank just before closing time and three masked men got out, walked into the place, forced their way into a couple of private vaults and ran off with a few thousand dollars, to say nothing of some valuable family plate."

"Right in broad daylight?" asked Jim.

"Yes, bold as brass. It was all over so quickly that the police didn't have a chance to do a thing about it. The bandits drove out of town before anything could be done in the way of turning in an alarm."

"They must have had the thing planned for a long time ahead, to pull off a stunt like that in the daytime," Don said. "They must be a slick bunch, to drive out of town in a car in broad daylight."

The supper bell rang at that moment and they went downstairs, to find the corps buzzing with the news from town. Nothing else was talked of during the meal, for such things were unusual and it was the first time in its history that Portville had come in for such distinction. Scores of different plans for catching the bandits were advanced, some of which made the colonel smile.

"Too bad the authorities don't request that you boys be put on the trail to run the outlaws down," he suggested.

"If we were put on the job we'd do our best to catch those thieves," Lieutenant Thompson boasted.

After the drill the cadets managed to straggle down into town to see if there was anything unusual, but they were disappointed. A number of the local police stood about, but that was the only sign that anything was wrong. Of course there were the extra knots of townspeople who buzzed and hummed, but as most of their talk was fruitless speculation the cadets paid no attention to it.

On the following day the Portville paper carried a screaming account of the robbery, in fact, there was little else in the paper but the news. Beside a dozen different accounts of the affair, given by the cashier and the clerks who had been eye-witnesses of the holdup, there were accounts of the activities of the police and promises for a speedy capture of the bandits. Pictures of the bank adorned the inside sheets, and the history of the institution took up an entire page.

It was Jim who found a paragraph of unusual interest in the account. Most of the cadets had contented themselves with a glance at the headlines of the paper, but Jim had taken the trouble to read the details. He lost no time in finding Don and Terry.

"Look here," he commanded them, pointing to the paper. "I just found one item of interest to us. Did you fellows know that the private vault of the Gates family was robbed?"

"I had heard so," Terry nodded. "Anything of value taken?"

"Yes, some very expensive silver plate. But this is what the paragraph says: 'Besides a quantity of silver plate and some family heirlooms in the way of jewelry, a silver cup trophy, won at school by Arthur Gates, was also taken from the family vault.'"

"A silver cup, eh?" said Don, his eyes narrowing. "Now,

can that be our silver cup?"

"Nope, it must be Gates'," grinned Terry.

"You know what I mean," rejoined Don, impatiently. "We thought that the friend from Canada took the cup back with him. Well, we may have been wrong all along, and Gates probably put it in the safe deposit vault at the bank."

"I guess that is what happened," Jim agreed. "Gates figured that we would think it went to Canada and would give up the search for it. And all the time it was right here in the town!"

"I think we had better show this article to the colonel," decided Don. "If the police ever do catch these men we may be able to see the cup before Gates gets it back."

The colonel was of the same opinion. "It may be another cup, of course," he warned. "Gates went to other schools and he may have won other cups. I hope more honestly than he won the 1933 cup. But if we get a chance we'll surely take a look at the cup the bandits took."

It was a foregone conclusion that it would take months to catch the bandits and no one had much faith in the Portville police. But with brilliant swiftness the local police caught the bandit trio. Working on the theory that the man had only pretended to flee in some nearby woods the local representatives of the law combed the thickets thoroughly, to run down their astonished quarry in less than a week. The three men were surprised in bed in a lonely cabin in the nearby hills, and the entire proceeds of the bank robbery were found with them.

It developed later that the three men planned to bury the plate and divide the money, hoping to split up and leave the region singly, but the prompt work of the town police effectively prevented that. They were swiftly brought to justice and the first inkling that the cadets had of the fact was when the morning newspaper arrived at the school.

"Well, what do you know about that!" murmured Terry, as they scanned the paper. "I didn't know the local police force had it in them."

"They surprised everyone, perhaps even themselves," smiled Don.

Jim was reading the account closely. "All of the effects of the Gates family were recovered," he announced. "The cup is mentioned here again, but there is no description of it. I certainly would like to know what cup it is."

"I guess we should be able to find out," said Don. "Suppose we go down to the newspaper office and hunt up the reporter that took the account? Surely he should be able to tell us something about the cup, for it is more than probable that he saw it."

At their earliest opportunity they went to town and to the newspaper office, where they asked for the reporter who had taken down the account of the robbery. He was a young man of a pleasant personality and he was very willing to talk to them.

"Just what is it that you want to know, boys?" he asked.

"In the account that you wrote up of the robbery you detailed the articles stolen from the different vaults," Don said. "We saw that among the effects taken from the Gates family vault there was a silver cup mentioned. Did you see that cup?"

"Yes," responded the reporter. "I saw all of the recovered articles. The cup was among them."

"What did it look like?" Don asked, trying not to appear too interested.

"Why do you want to know?" countered the reporter.

"Mr. Gates won several cups in his school days, and he won one at Woodcrest," Don answered. "We were just wondering if it was the Woodcrest cup that was stolen."

The boys, when planning their method of procedure before coming to the newspaper office, had decided on that story. The reporter was satisfied at once.

"Why, I can't tell you that exactly," he said, slowly. "I didn't notice anything but the date on it."

"What was the date?" Terry asked quickly.

"The date was 1933," was the answer.

"That was the Woodcrest cup," nodded Don. "We were wondering up at the school, and we three fellows decided to stop in and see if that was the cup. Thanks a lot."

"That is perfectly all right," the reporter smiled. "Shall I ask Mr. Gates sometime if that was the cup?"

"No, it won't be necessary," Don replied, casually. "We know that it is the cup he won at Woodcrest, because he won one in that year. I suppose he locked it up in the vault again?"

"No!" was the unexpected reply. "He left all of the other valuables there, but he took the cup back to his home with him!"

"Maybe he feels so much pride in it that he wants it at hand," suggested Jim as a venture.

"I don't know, I'm sure, but I know that he took it home

with him," the reporter concluded.

When they had thanked him once more the boys left the office and started back to school, talking the situation over between them.

"Well, the cup is still in our midst, and we may have another try at it," Don remarked.

"As long as it is at the house, yes," agreed Jim. "Maybe he feels that it will be safest where he can keep an eye on it."

"Um," observed Terry, sarcastically. "All we have to do is to get in and get at it!"

"Something may turn up and give us the chance," said Don, hopefully. "You never can tell."

Chapter 19
A Conversation in the Dark

Early one February morning a committee of ladies and gentlemen waited on Colonel Morrell. He saw them come up the drive, and was surprised to note that the group was made up of a clergyman, two well-known businessmen, and two ladies whom he knew to be leaders of women's activities in Portville. When they had all been seated in his office, the clergyman, a fine, straight-forward young man who was making good in the largest church in the town, broached the subject to him.

"Colonel Morrell," began Dr. Bicknell. "You may be a bit surprised to see such a formidable gathering bear down on you, but I assure you that we have good intentions. I don't know whether you have heard anything about it or not, but on Washington's Birthday Portville is to celebrate its small but honored share in the events of the Revolutionary War. We are a committee in charge of arrangements and have come to ask you for you co-operation on that day. The center of attraction will be the old Gannon House and the picturization of the stirring events that happened in it."

"The Gannon House?" asked the colonel. "I've heard of it, but I don't just recall where it is."

"It is the house at present occupied by Mr. Melvin Gates and his family. You know the place now?"

"Oh, yes, surely," affirmed the colonel. "Now I do remember. That is the most historic house in Portville, eh?"

"Yes," replied Dr. Bicknell. "At the time of the Revolution our armies were harried by one particular spy who seemed to find out every move that the Continental Army made. At last this spy was run down by two determined citizens of Portville, and was found to be a young teacher who lodged at the Gannon House. He was taken from the house by indignant patriots and hanged just outside the town. The act was most fortunate, for from that moment there was no more leaking of news to the British.

"On Washington's Birthday we propose to have a pageant which will show most of that, all but the actual hanging, which

99

people can dispense with, I imagine. The events leading up to the capture of the British spy were highly dramatic, and we wish to show them in the pageant, which will take place in the daytime. What we want you to do, Colonel Morrell, is to permit your boys to parade in the morning. There will be a parade of ex-service men, fraternal organizations and business clubs, to say nothing of the patriotic organizations, and we feel that the line of march would not be complete unless your splendid boys marched with us."

"In the name of the cadet corps, I thank you," acknowledged the colonel. "I shall be most happy to have the cadet units march in the parade. The boys haven't been in a public parade for a number of years and it would do them good to get in one. Yes, I shall be very happy to allow the boys to parade."

"That is very helpful, and we are grateful to you for your co-operation," smiled the pleasant young pastor. "Now, there is one other thing we would like to request. In the evening there will be a public inspection of the Gannon House and at that time we would like to post some of your cadets at various points about the house, to act as guides or whatever else may come up. Can you see your way clear to let us use a few of your honor pupils, say one at the front and rear doors, and one on each side and the staircases? That will add an impressive tone to the whole thing."

"Yes, that can be easily done," promised the colonel. "I shall be glad to help in any way possible. I shall detail my captains and lieutenants to take posts in the house and do whatever else you wish them to do."

The members of the committee once more thanked the colonel, and after a few plans were made they left him. In due time the news was circulated among the corps and the cadets looked forward with more or less pleasure to the event.

"It will be something different," Terry expressed it. "Won't I enjoy marching through town, the center of all eyes."

"You mean the town will be the center of all eyes?" asked Jim, slyly.

"No, dope! I will be!"

"If I remember correctly, you will be perched on the rear of a gun carriage," retorted Jim. "But just think of me, my boy! I'll be sitting on a horse, the captain of the cavalry, as proud as you please, bowing to the ladies."

"With all due respect to your exalted position," grinned

Terry. "I would advise you not to bow too much. You might tumble over the neck of the horse and bump your nose!"

"I guess I'll be the only one who won't shine at all," said Don. "I'm just a poor, plain little infantry soldier! A lieutenant on foot doesn't show up much."

"I thought that Gates' house looked like a very old one when we were in it," said Don. "But I never guessed that it had such a history. Now that we know the history we can account for the huge doors, the massive bolts and the wide, spreading staircase."

An account in the newspaper interested the boys. It related how, at a time when the British raided Portville, the Gannon family took their silver plate and buried it out in the garden. The British had stolen everything in sight, but the silver was later dug up by the members of the family and saved.

"I'd like to see the spot where it was buried, sometime," said Terry. "That must have been an interesting sight. Imagine the men out in the garden in the dead of night, burying the boxes of silver plate!"

Parade orders were given two days before Washington's Birthday and the cadets found themselves in for a busy time. Dress uniforms were brought out and cleaned, swords polished and bayonets rubbed down. Rifles were inspected and the horses well groomed, for the colonel was anxious for his boys to give a good account of themselves.

Good fortune fell to Jim. As an officer he had received a post inside the historic house. In high spirits he told Don and Terry of his good fortune.

"Nice going, kid!" approved Don, generously. "Where is your post to be?"

Jim made a wry face. "I'm not so sure that the post is a good one, for I am stationed at the back door. I won't be able to see much of what goes on there, but at least I'll be in the house."

"Maybe we're luckier than you are, at that," chuckled the red-headed boy. "Those of us who are not to be on post in the house will be able to roam around the town, for the colonel has given us full liberty on that day. But just the same, I think I'd rather be in the house."

"So should I," nodded Don. "At any rate, keep your eyes open, Jim. There is no telling what you may see."

"I'll do that," Jim promised.

On Washington's Birthday the school showed the marks of feverish activity. After breakfast and the school exercises the corps assembled on the campus. It was indeed a splendid sight. The cavalry, with Captain Jim and Lieutenant Thompson at the head, assembled on the road in front of the campus, while the cadet brigade took up the campus. Back of the infantry the artillery unit stood at attention, the several guns polished to the last degree. All of the cadets were in dress uniform, with the tall military hats, the braided coats, and the white gloves. When the corps was fully formed and the orders of the day read, they started out to join the other divisions of the parade, the citizen units.

With the jangle of trappings the cavalry, in perfect formation four abreast, moved off down the road, and the infantry, also marching four abreast, with the band playing a lively march and the heels of the young men ringing out on the pavement, followed. A dull rumble to the rear marked the progress of the artillery division. When they struck the center of town they fell into place behind the patriotic clubs. The parade began at eleven o'clock.

It was a fine parade from start to finish. A number of ex-service men led the van, with the town organizations following. They made up fully one-half of the parade and then came the Woodcrest Military Institute corps. Afterward, everyone gave praise to the young soldiers from the school up in the hills. The cavalry was superb, the infantry marched with precision, every foot in step and every white glove swinging with accuracy, the flags drooping colorfully and the young men erect. The field guns rolled along looking grim and effective, and when the parade finally came to an end the colonel was more than satisfied.

In the afternoon the pageant was held and the cadets, no longer under orders, watched the display. Fortunately, the Gannon House stood back from the street and was favored with wide lawns, and the people who came to see the spectacle, and that included practically the entire town, were all able to see the display. Actors dressed in the costumes of Revolutionary times took part and it proved to be most entertaining. A young man came to the door of the Gannon House, dressed in the Colonial costume, and asked for lodging, explaining that he was a teacher and wanted to earn his living in the town. He was graciously received by the Gannon family and installed as one of the family. But no sooner had this young man settled himself than he began to entertain strange visitors. Very erect men visited him, listening to his low-spoken talk with great attention and then going away. At night the teacher left the house, wrapped in a great cloak, explaining to Mr. Gannon, who asked his purpose, that he was merely walking for exercise and recreation. Then came two patriots who pretended great friendship for the young teacher and watched him at night, crouching beneath the windows to do so. Toward the end of the pageant they unmasked the spy and Mr. Gannon was the first to condemn him to the fate of hanging. The last scene showed the Gannon family hearing from the lips of American officers that no more information was "leaking" to the British.

The pageant was well given and the spectators enjoyed it. Gates' house was then opened to the public for a supper, which was served to the members of the committee. At eight o'clock the doors were formally opened to the general public, and Jim took his post at the back door.

Hudson, as senior captain of the corps, occupied the central position at the front door. Other captains and lieutenants had posts throughout the house. There were two cadets on the lower floor, one in the center of the house and another in the huge, Colonial kitchen, a cadet on the central staircase and one on the landing of the second floor. One cadet stood post on the third floor, where the quarters of the servants still stood unchanged since the days of the building of the house. And at the back door stood Jim.

He was not sure that his post was the best in the world, but he did have an active one. Early in the evening numbers of townsfolk, some of them brilliantly dressed, entered the house and were led through it by members of the Daughters of the American Revolution, who were all dressed in costumes of that period. When they finished inspecting the house they went to the grounds in the back and kept Jim active. When he heard a step on the other side of the door he would step quickly to the door, open it wide and step back, holding it open until the persons had passed through and then closing it. The yard had been lighted only in the immediate vicinity of the house. The back gardens remained in darkness.

Of course much was seen of the Gates family. Melvin Gates, who had recovered from his accident, was everywhere in evidence, easily the center of the affair. A few knew that the senior Gates was more than delighted at the entire circumstance, as it was raising him vastly in the eyes of the townspeople in general. He had not himself offered his house for inspection, but had been very willing when the subject had been broached to him by the leaders of the movement. Arthur Gates was also much in the public eye as he moved with immense sociability around the house, his wife beside him, bowing and smiling. When the party happened to be composed of persons of wealth and distinction in Portville the bow and the smile became very genial indeed.

However, not only the rich and influential came that night to the old Gannon House, but also the poor and humble. Many a plain working man, interested in the history of his country or the structure of the house, came to look through it and Jim opened the door to such as well as to the others who swept by him with a swish of costly garments. To all of them Jim extended the same unfailing courtesy.

Toward nine o'clock in the evening a man who looked to be a laborer passed out of the back door and went into the garden. Jim noted that the man looked at his watch and then seemed to be waiting. After a time he went down to the gardens, losing himself in the blackness beyond the electric lights.

Not fifteen minutes after he had gone there was another step inside the kitchen and Jim quickly opened the door. Arthur Gates stepped out, looked all around him without paying any attention to Jim, and then set off at a rapid pace for the garden, following the same direction taken by the man. Jim was curious at once.

"I'd like to know what is going on," he reflected. "I wonder if I ought to go down and see? Very few people are coming through any more, and besides, if I do leave my post, it will be thought I did so to run an errand. I guess I'll take a chance on it."

Seeing that no one was about Jim slipped quickly to the side of the yard and away from the glare of the lights. Then, following a path which wound down into the farther reaches of the place he moved forward, treading with infinite care, avoiding gravelled walks where possible and fairly creeping over them when they could not be avoided. In a short time he reached the garden and saw ahead of him in the darkness two forms.

A screen of bushes loomed between him and the two men

and Jim crouched as he made his way to them. Once in their shelter he was able to hear plainly what was being said.

"—close against the back wall," Gates was saying.

"You want me to mark the spot so you'll know the place?" the man asked.

"No," replied Gates. "I don't care if I never see it again."

"Not valuable, eh?" the man asked, cautiously.

"No, only a trinket I won at school, but I'm sick and tired of having it around. It is better off buried. But never mind that; all you have to do is to bury the thing. I don't want it done by daylight, either. Will you do it tomorrow night?"

"Sure, around ten o'clock. I got to work up until that time. Right here will be all right eh?" the laborer said.

"Yes. I'll pay you well for it, but you are to keep your mouth shut. Good heavens! this thing you're to bury isn't worth a dollar, and yet I've had more trouble with it than if it cost a thousand. Now, let's get back and you be sure to go to work tomorrow night."

With that they separated and Jim could see them going toward the house, but the laborer branched off and left the grounds while Arthur Gates went in the back door. Before he went to his post again Jim looked carefully around the garden where he stood. There was a high wall nearby and he knew that he was at the end of the property.

Then he went back to his post, taking care to approach it from the side of the house, casually and as though he was coming from an errand. Once more he took up his post at the back door.

"So Gates is going to bury the cup?" he reflected. "And it had given as much trouble as though it cost a thousand dollars. Of course, it may not be the cup, after all, but I'll bet it is. Well, we'll just dig it up as soon as he gets it planted!"

In another hour all inspection of the Gannon House was over and it once more became simply the home of the Gates family. The cadets on post assembled and marched up to the school reporting in from duty, and soon after that Jim was relating his remarkable story to Don and Terry.

Chapter 20
The Digger in the Garden

"This must be the place!"

Jim whispered it cautiously and the two shadows with him nodded silently. Don and Terry crouched down beside him behind the high wall which ran back of the home of Arthur Gates.

It was on the following night, and three cadets were there with the full permission of Colonel Morrell. Jim, after his talk with his friends, had gone straight to the headmaster with the story. The colonel had also been of the opinion that it was the cup that Gates planned to bury. He agreed that it would be best for them to watch the digging and to get the object at once, before the time elapsing would give the ground a chance to freeze. So the three cadets crouched behind the wall bordering Gates' place on this February night.

"You think this is the right spot?" Don whispered.

"Yes," returned Jim. "What time is it?"

Terry consulted a watch with a lighted dial. "Just five minutes of ten," he replied. "We got here just in time."

They had reached the property a few minutes before and had skirted the wall, halting at the place which Jim had believed to be opposite the spot where Gates and the man had conferred on the previous night. They straightened up and Jim reached upward, finding that he was just able to place his fingertips on the top of the wall.

"Give me a boost up," he ordered.

Don cupped his hand and by the aid of this step Jim sprang onto the wall. For a moment there was silence as he peered down into the garden inside, and then he leaned toward them.

"This is the place," he whispered. "Come on up."

Terry formed the step by which Don joined his brother on the wall and then they both pulled the red-head up. Jim then looked carefully back of him.

"There are no lights back of us," he said. "I'm pretty sure that no one can see us."

They settled themselves to wait and the minutes dragged by. It seemed an age, though it was in reality only fifteen minutes when Terry hissed warningly.

"Somebody is coming!"

They crouched low as they saw a bobbing light coming down the path toward them. It was a man with a lantern and as he drew nearer they saw that it was a short man, whom Jim recognized as the man who had talked with Gates. Near the wall the man halted, and placed a wooden box on the ground. Setting the lantern down, and without looking around him, he dropped a pick and shovel from his shoulder. He took up the pick, raised it above his head and brought it down with a thump on the hard earth.

The boys, when talking the situation over at school, were agreed that Gates had received his idea from the newspaper account of the burying of the silver plate by the Gannon family. When they saw the wooden box on the ground they were firmly convinced that it held the disputed silver cup, for it was just the right size.

The digger in the garden worked steadily at his task, breaking the stiff earth with his pick and then shovelling it away with his shovel. He had made a hole perhaps three feet deep when something wholly unexpected happened.

There was a sudden flash of fire back of the watching cadets and they were bathed in an embarrassing glow of light. Turning startled heads over their shoulders they saw that a garage nearby had caught fire and that a pan of oil was blazing up to the sky. The man working in the garden looked up with a grunt of fright, but fortunately not in their immediate direction, for the glare was spreading and he looked slightly to one side of them. Seeing how things stood the three cadets dropped from the wall swiftly and with as little noise as possible, crouching at the bottom of the wall outside Gates' property. The glare died down abruptly.

"Did he see us?" questioned Don, eagerly.

"No," whispered Jim. "But that was a narrow escape."

"You bet," agreed Terry. "There we were, sitting on the wall like three chickens! That was a lucky escape."

"We had better wait here until he finishes his digging," Jim suggested. "Listen; he has gone back to work."

They could hear the man resume his digging. But it was unfortunate that they could not see into the garden, for real trouble was coming their way rapidly.

Arthur Gates, uneasy over the affair, had been standing

107

at an upper window when the flare had illuminated the sky, and clearly and distinctly he had seen the three cadets on the wall. Uttering an exclamation the man ran from the house and made his way to the digger. Unknown to the boys a rapid interchange of words followed and then Gates took up the box and went back to the house. The man who was doing the digging dropped his shovel and waited a moment, until he was joined by the caretaker of the property. Some whispering passed between them and then they silently made their way to a gate in the wall.

The three cadets crouched there in the blackness of the night beside the wall and waited. They strained their ears to hear continued sounds of the digging but they heard nothing.

"He must be finished," Terry whispered.

"I should think that we would hear him replacing the dirt," suggested Jim.

"Suppose you go aloft and see?" said Don, in a low voice.

Jim straightened up and Don gave him a hand to the top of the wall. Once there Jim peered carefully over to see how far the man had gotten in his work. But in a moment he was down again.

"The man is gone!" he told them, in wonder.

"Then he has finished," concluded Don, but Jim shook his head.

"I don't know why he should be. The lantern is still there and the hole is open, but the box is gone!"

"Gone?" the others cried guardedly.

"Yes, and I don't see a sign of the man," Jim replied.

"Let me take a look," Don directed briefly.

When he had been hoisted up he made the same observation that Jim had. The three boys were puzzled.

"Confound that fire!" growled Terry. "If it hadn't been for that we would know what was going on."

"It doesn't look very good to me," observed Jim.

They waited for a moment, undecided as to what to do. The only sound that reached their ears was the sound of men in the nearby garage, who had put out the unexpected fire and who were talking about it. They were not near enough to cause the cadets any misgivings, however.

"Give me another boost," said Don, but Jim caught his arm in a firm grasp.

"Listen!" commanded his brother.

There had been a faint sound near them, along the wall, the sound as of a small stick breaking. There was no further noise but they had heard that one plainly. A suspicion leaped into Don's mind.

"Maybe someone saw us and they are after us," he whispered.

No sooner had he spoken than two distinct shadows loomed up before them along the wall.

"Run, you guys!" cried Jim.

They dashed away from the wall as fast as they could go toward the open field, the two men hard at their heels. Jim and Terry were slightly ahead of Don and running swiftly, breaking their way recklessly through the bushes that barred their way. Don had been a bit slower but was sufficiently ahead of his pursuers to keep him out of danger. They ran in the general direction of the school, trusting to luck to keep them out of holes and other pitfalls.

But Don was the unlucky one. Jim and Terry veered to the right across the fields but Don kept on going, failing to follow their lead closely. When he noticed that they had changed their course he swung around to follow them. There was nothing ahead of him, but as he ran forward he felt himself flung back abruptly, to tumble breathless to the ground. Before him was a long chicken run, with high chicken wire strung from pole to pole to pole, and Don had run against this net in the dark, to be playfully tossed for a considerable loss.

It proved to be a fatal loss. Just as he scrambled to his feet the two men swooped down on him and two pairs of strong arms gripped him. He struggled but the men held him fast.

"Let go of me," he demanded, somewhat breathlessly.

"Nothing doing, bub," growled the man who had been digging. "You come along with us."

"Where are you taking me?" Don asked, as they led him along.

"Back to the house," replied the other, an older man. "We want to find out what you were doing snooping around there. I'm caretaker at the house and I can have you arrested for trespassing."

Don had a pretty fair idea that Arthur Gates would not have him arrested but he realized that he was in a tough spot.

Chapter 21
The Cup at Last

There was nothing more said until they reached the house, where Don was quickly ushered into the presence of Arthur Gates. The man was seated in the library when they entered, with a book in his hand, and he looked up in apparent surprise when Don was brought in.

"What is this, Garry?" he asked of the caretaker.

"Caught this fellow trespassing on the grounds, sir," said the caretaker.

"You did not!" denied Don. "You caught me way over in the next field."

"But you must have been on the grounds, in order for Garry to have seen you," declared Gates, putting his book down. He looked keenly at Don. "Why, you are one of the cadets from Woodcrest, aren't you?"

"Yes," nodded Don. "I am."

"What are you doing out at this late hour?" asked Gates. "Taking French leave, I suppose?"

"Yes," said Don, seeing his course.

"You should be in bed by this time at the school," Gates went on. "What were you doing on my property?"

"I haven't been on your property yet," said Don.

"The wall is my property," flashed Gates.

"Oh, so you saw me on the wall?" questioned Don.

Gates bit his lip. He had not intended to say so much. "Never mind who saw you there; you were there." He turned to the other two. "You may go now." To the laborer he said: "I won't need you any more tonight, Tom. Drop around to see me in the morning."

The two men went out and Gates turned to Don once more. "Now, young man, what is your name?"

"Mercer," replied Don.

"What were you snooping around here for tonight, Mercer?"

"Three of us were out on a lark and we looked over your wall on the way back," replied Don.

"You were sitting on the wall," accused Gates.

"Yes, we sat on the wall," confessed Don. "But we didn't trespass on your property and so you can't hold us. All you can do is report us to the colonel."

"I think you were prowling around here for something else, young man," growled Gates, rising.

"What for?" asked Don, looking straight into Gates' eyes.

"How should I know?" the man evaded. "I'm going to take you into custody for a time at least, Mercer. You come with me."

"Where are you taking me?" Don asked, as Gates took hold of his arm.

"Never mind asking so many questions, but come along. Don't make any resistance or I shall call in the police. By the way, aren't you one of those cadets who brought in my father from that accident?"

"Yes," acknowledged Don.

"Too bad you had to mix yourself up in this business."

"What business are you talking about?" asked Don pointedly.

"Never mind that. What became of your companions?"

"I suppose they got away."

"Well, I'll find out who they were and have them punished, too. Now, out this way."

Curiously Don followed his captor out into the hall and up the big staircase to the second floor, down that hall and up a flight of stairs to the third floor. Coming to a door there Gates opened it and thrust Don inside, closing the door after him. A moment later and Don heard a key rattle in the lock. Then the sound of rapidly retreating footsteps came to his ears.

He attempted to move around the room and bumped into something sharp that poked into his waist. Striking a match that he found in his pocket, Don saw that he was in a billiard room and that he had bumped the table. Seeing a light switch on the wall he moved toward it and turned on the lights. Then he looked curiously around his prison.

There were no windows in the room, but a skylight gave it illumination in the daytime. If necessary Don was sure that he could jump from the table to the skylight and make his way to the roof, but he had no intention of trying it at present. Instead, he went to the door and tried it carefully, finding it locked.

"They won't keep me in here long," he thought grimly. "I'll

raise such a racket that he'll be glad to let me out. But I wonder if that will be the best thing to do?"

He began to shake the door, to try its strength, and at last pressed against the lock with all his strength. Although that had no effect on the lock directly it had an unexpected outcome. There was a step out in the hall, and the key was turned in the lock. When the door was thrown open Don stared into the face of a butler.

He was the first one to recover himself. "Oh, thanks a lot for opening the door," he said, carelessly, seeing his way out. "Someone must have turned the key in the lock."

"But what—who are you, sir?" the surprised butler stammered.

"I'm an acquaintance of Mr. Gates," said Don. "I came up here with him and he left me to go down stairs. Someone must have turned the lock while I was in here."

"But, sir," protested the butler. "No one has been past this door. I sleep in the next room and I came out before going to bed because I heard you rattle the door."

"And that was very kind of you," said Don. He saw that the butler was not overly bright and that he would probably have no trouble with the man. "It must have been an accident, my getting locked in here. Well, I'll go downstairs and join Mr. Gates. Thank you very much."

"You are very welcome, sir. But—"

"But what?" inquired Don, frowning at the man. "Do you think I am a burglar, man? Can't you see the uniform I have on? I'm a cadet at Woodcrest School."

"No offense meant, sir," hastily replied the butler. "It was just—hum—irregular, sir, and I wondered. Goodnight, sir."

"Goodnight," responded Don, hoping that Gates had not heard the talking.

Apparently he had not, for there was no movement as he walked cautiously down to the second floor. The butler had gone back to his room and no one was in the hall. The young cadet was undecided as to what to do now that he was free.

"I ought to make a good effort to get hold of that cup, now that I am in the house," he reasoned. "But I don't know how to go about it."

He tiptoed along the second floor hall, determined to go to the lower floor and look around down there for the cup. He was not greatly worried about the whole situation for he knew that the colonel was back of him in whatever he did, and even in the event that the Gates family got highhanded about things he was sure that the significant word spoken to them would serve to cool their temper. So he had some degree of comfort in the fact that it would probably come out right in the end. And when he stopped to think of the heavy injustice that George Long had suffered all these years because of the flagrant villainy of these same people he had no scruples against prowling around Gates' house.

A light showed under the door of the room into which the cadets had carried Melvin Gates the night of the accident and Don stopped there, struck by an idea. He moved up close to the door and listened, being rewarded by the murmur of voices inside. Although they were pitched in a low key he was nevertheless able to make out what was being said.

"But you cannot keep that young man a prisoner," he heard Melvin Gates say.

"Well, what am I going to do with him?" his son asked impatiently.

"I do not know, Arthur. You think he was prowling around to find that cup?"

"Oh, of course!" cried the son, wearily. "That cup has cost me more anxiety than anything I ever had anything to do with in my life!"

"That is entirely your own fault, Arthur. If you had not been so dishonest all of your life you wouldn't be in such a fix."

"Don't preach to me, father," snapped the son, angrily.

"It is too bad I didn't preach to you when you were smaller, instead of filling your pockets with money that you didn't have the sense to take care of. Where is the cup now?"

"I threw it in the closet in my study, at the end of the hall," was the answer, which sent a thrill of hope through Don.

There was a rustle inside the room, much as though someone was getting out of bed. "Tomorrow we'll dispose of that cup by melting it in the furnace," said the elder Gates. "Wait until I get a bathrobe on and we'll go up and interview that young man in the billiard room."

Don waited to hear no more. Arthur Gates had given him the clue he needed and like a shot he darted off down the hall to the room at the end. This was the room which tallied with the brief description the man had given, but Don poked his head carefully in the door before entering, as he did not wish to walk into anyone's bedroom.

But it was a small study which lay before him. In the dim light which flooded in from the hall he could see the outline of a table, an easy chair and a pile of books on the table. On the other side of the room he made out a door. He entered the room and made his way to it, finding it slightly open. At that moment he heard the two Gates leave the room of the older man and begin to mount the stairs to the third floor.

Don's groping hands encountered a wooden box on the floor of the closet. It seemed to be the same size as the one which had been in the garden that night, and as there was no other object on the floor or on the single shelf he was sure that he had at last come across the 1933 class trophy.

"I've got the cup at last," he reflected. "Now, the big job is to get out of this house!"

Chapter 22
Direct Action

Terry and Jim ran with all the speed they could muster across the fields, believing that Don was close behind them.

But Jim finally realized that no one was close to them and he came to a halt, calling to Terry in a low tone. The red-headed boy stopped and joined him.

"Did we lose our pursuers?" Terry panted.

"Yes," gasped Jim, gulping in the fresh air. "And I'm afraid that we have lost Don!"

"Isn't he around?" cried Terry.

"No. I don't know what has happened to him. I heard him pounding along after us and then I lost the sound. Maybe he just branched off in another direction."

"Let's give him the old signal," urged Terry, puckering up his lips. He whistled in a low, penetrating note, the signal which had always been known to the three friends and which had been agreed upon before they had left on their night's quest. The sound went across the fields but there was no answer, though they strained their ears to listen.

"I wonder if those men caught Don?" said Jim.

"Oh, I don't think so," reassured Terry. "I guess he just got separated from us. Before we came out we agreed to meet under the lamp post in case we got separated. Let's go over to the street and see if he is waiting there."

Together they crossed the lots and emerged on the street upon which the Gannon House faced, approaching the lamp light with some degree of caution. But after they had waited in the shadow of a tree for ten minutes they were both forced to the same conclusion.

"Not a doubt in the world that he was captured," sighed Terry.

"I'm afraid so," agreed Jim. "If he had gone off in another direction he would surely have come here directly. At this moment he must be a prisoner in Gates' house."

"What are we going to do about it?" demanded Terry practically.

"What can we do?" asked Jim helplessly.

"I think we need a little direct action," said Terry. "Let's go back to the house and see if we can get a look at him. We may even be able to set him free."

"OK, I'm willing," responded Jim, moving off down the street. "Perhaps they have turned him over to the police."

"That isn't likely to do them any good," explained Terry. "We have the colonel back of us and have nothing to worry about. Anyway, I think that Don will drop a word or two that will give 'em something to think about."

"Take it easy now," warned Jim, as they drew close to the gate before the big house. "No telling who is snooping around the grounds."

Seeing no one in immediate range of vision they flitted across the sidewalk and entered the grounds of the old place. Keeping close to the hedge they made their way along it up to the house and then paused.

"Lights are none too plentiful in the house," whispered Terry.

There was only one lighted room in the downstairs. A low light burned in a bedroom on the second floor and two rooms were lighted on the third floor. With one accord, after a hasty glance around, the two cadets crept to the window and looked under the shade into the library.

"No one in there," Jim whispered.

The room was empty. A single reading lamp burned in the place but there was no sign of life. At that moment Terry nudged his companion's arm.

"Say! Doesn't something occur to you?"

"No," said Jim. "What?"

"It was under this same window that the patriots stood and saw that spy school teacher talking with British officers!"

"Gee, that's right," mused Jim. "But we have one consolation. The Gates' won't take Don out and hang him!"

"No," agreed Terry, with a half chuckle. "But they'll want to do it to us if they catch us around here."

"You missed your cue," grinned Jim. "You should have said that we are doing all the hanging around here!"

"Oof! Bad pun," snorted Terry. "But what are we going to do now?"

"Golly, I don't know," admitted Jim. "There is no question that Don is in the house, and that we have got to get in and rescue him. But how the devil are we to do it?"

"Don't know how many of my ancestors were burglars!" said Terry, grimly. "But let's see how we stand in regard to windows."

He reached up and pushed on the frame of the window but found that it was locked. He tried another with the same result.

"Careless people!" he grunted. "Leave their windows locked every night!"

"Perhaps we can find one open on the other side of the house," suggested Jim. "Suppose we take a look."

They passed around the back of the house, but just as Jim turned the corner of the kitchen pantry he stopped and crouched down, pulling his companion with him.

"What's up?" Terry whispered.

"Caretaker prowling around," returned Jim. "Keep still, he's coming this way."

The form of a man loomed up before them and they held their breath as the man passed within five feet of them. When he had turned the corner of the house back of them they breathed in relief.

"Narrow escape, that," commented Chucklehead.

"Yeah," agreed Jim. "Well, I guess he has gone around to the other side of the house. Lucky thing he didn't come and catch us under the window. Let's look this side over before he returns."

They crept along the side of the house, examining windows and testing them, but they were all firm. At last the two friends drew back under a tree.

"It's no use," groaned Jim. "We can't get into the house."

"It would be a rough joke on us if Don wasn't in there, after all," commented the disappointed Terry.

"But he must be. Too bad we can't get at the second floor windows. Surely a bedroom window must be open."

"No doubt. But who wants to climb into a bedroom, to have a lady yell blue murder or get shot at?"

"I hope it wouldn't be as bad as all that. Say! This tree arches right over that porch roof!"

Jim had been looking up into the branches of the tree thoughtfully and now his friend followed his gaze. He saw that the tree, which grew so close to the house, extended at least two strong limbs a few feet over the roof of the porch shelter.

"There isn't any reason why we shouldn't climb this tree

and drop onto the roof," Terry said. "There are four windows that we can reach."

"Yes, and the roof can't be seen from the street," Jim pointed out. "Think we had better go to it?"

"Yes, I do. The trunk of the tree isn't so big that we can't climb it. But I'm afraid that we'll get our uniforms fearfully dirty, because we'll have to take off our overcoats to climb."

"Bother the uniforms!" cried Jim, impatiently. "We can have them cleaned. I'm going up."

"Wait until I take a look around, to see if the gentleman is still taking a walk," suggested Terry. "Stay here and keep close to the tree until I get back."

With this final word the red-head glided off into the darkness and was lost to Jim's sight. Two or three minutes passed, and Jim was just growing restless, when young Mr. Mackson rejoined him.

"Coast is clear," he informed him. "The caretaker is around on the other side and just bound for the back garden. I don't think we'll be troubled with him. So here goes my overcoat."

Without wasting further time the cadets slipped out of their heavy coats and Terry dropped his carelessly on the ground nearby. But Jim shook his head at that.

"Don't leave the coats lying around here," he warned. "That fellow may be back at any time, and we don't want him to find the coats while we are up aloft."

"Good head you have, Jimmie boy," approved Terry. "Never thought it of you. Let's park them behind these bushes, close to the porch."

When the two boys had stowed the overcoats away so that there was no likely chance that they would be found, they returned to the foot of the tree and Terry gave Jim a boost as far up the tapering trunk as he could. From his shoulders Jim began his climb and stuck doggedly to it until he reached a small limb below the level of the tin roof. Then he called down for Terry to follow him.

His friend had a much harder job of it because he had to start from the ground but he moved slowly and surely upward. It was some years since Terry had "shinnied" up a tree and he found it hard work, but, resting at intervals, he soon joined Jim at the small limb. Without words they moved on, and before long wormed their way out on a limb that hung suspended over the roof.

"Be awfully careful when you drop on that roof," whispered Jim. "Try to land on your toes and don't thump if you can help it."

Jim then swung down under the limb, hanging by his hands, and measured the distance to the roof. It was a matter of less than a foot, he discovered, and with his toes pointing downward he let go and dropped. There was scarcely a sound as he landed.

"Come on," he whispered.

Terry swung down under the limb and after a moment of steadying himself dropped to the roof. Jim steadied him as he landed and they stood together on the tin surface and looked around.

"Hooray, a partially opened window!" breathed Jim.

Close to them a window had been left open some few inches and they made their way to it quietly. Both of them felt a tingle of excitement.

"We'll want to get into the upper hall, if possible," said Terry, guardedly. "Let's hope this isn't a bedroom. What does it look like?"

Jim was in the lead and he peered into the room, finally raising the window noiselessly in order to see better. He turned to his waiting friend.

"It doesn't seem to be a bedroom," he informed him. "Looks more like some kind of a study. I can see a table and an armchair, and a little light comes in from the hall. I guess this is just the kind of a room we are looking for."

"Then let's get in and go a-snooping," urged Terry.

Jim raised the window fully and stepped into the room, Terry following closely at his heels. They paused to make out their surroundings, when Terry gripped Jim's arm tightly.

"Somebody in this room!" he hissed.

Before Jim could move someone stepped out of the closet and confronted them. For a single instant there was a silence that froze them, and then the light from the hall fell on the features of the one who stared at them.

"Don!" they whispered.

A sigh of pure relief broke from the one who had stepped out of the closet. "Boy, oh boy," Don returned. "You two fellows scared me out of a year's growth!"

"You gave us a mighty good start, too," returned Terry as they moved close to him. "What are you doing in here?"

"I have the cup!" Don replied.

"No fooling?" gasped Jim.

"Yes, it was in that closet. Listen, we have got to get out of here. The two Gates—"

A cry broke out on the third floor and a door slammed. They waited to hear no more.

"Quickly, out the window with you," cried Don. "We've got to clear this house on the double!"

Terry skipped through the window like lightning and Jim threw himself after him. Just before Don followed he could hear Arthur Gates roaring at the butler on the third floor. He joined his companions on the roof.

"Go on down and I'll toss the cup to you," he told Jim.

"Shall I take a chance by dropping off the roof?" asked Jim.

"No," said Don. "You might break a leg, and you don't know where you'll land."

Jim measured his distance and jumped up, catching the limb and swinging out on it with the agility of a monkey. He slid down the tree and dropped safely to the ground.

"Drop the cup," he called.

Don dropped the cup over the edge of the roof and it fell to the ground. It was still boxed and he had no fear that any harm would come to it. Terry was already in the tree and swinging down toward the ground.

Jim, leaning down to pick up the box, felt himself gripped by a strong hand, which fastened itself on his shoulder. Before he could cry out he was dragged upright, to find himself in the grasp of the caretaker. Terry landed at the foot of the tree and was immediately seized by the other hand of the man. So taken by surprise were they that for the moment they uttered no sound.

"Goodnight!" flashed through the mind of the red-headed boy. "The end of a perfect day!"

120

Chapter 23
The Mystery Is Solved

It was a black moment for the two cadets in the grasp of the caretaker.

With the cup in their possession and the task to which they had set themselves almost successfully completed it was little short of heartbreaking to miss the mark in this fashion. The man who held them was a big and powerful man and they knew by the iron grip upon their shoulders that resistance was out of the question. It was possible for them to put up a fight, of course, but it would probably take them so long that the entire effort would be useless.

Terry was the first to recover his wits. The man who held them was not looking up into the tree; he looked in grim satisfaction at them and apparently had no knowledge of the presence of Don above him. Terry realized that the other must be warned quickly.

"Well, Mr. Caretaker," he said, loudly. "You seem to have taken my friend and me prisoners. What are you going to do about it?"

"I'm going to run you kids down to the town lockup in a mighty big hurry and put you behind the bars for housebreaking," the man replied.

A very slight scraping noise in the tree above them ceased abruptly as the sound of the different voices could be heard on the night air. For a second there was an agony of doubt in Terry's mind, but the man did not look up.

"You can't prove that we were housebreaking," said Jim, the idea suddenly dawning upon him.

"I can't, heh?" snorted the man. "Then why else—"

The sentence was never completed. Something big and heavy that closely resembled a boy in a gray uniform shot down out of the tree, landing with all force upon the shoulders of the caretaker. Under the impact of Don's body the man fell forward, losing his hold on the shoulders of Jim and Terry. Don went down too, but was up like a shot.

"Beat it as fast as you can!" he cried, seeing that Jim had

the box in his hand.

"The overcoats!" cried Jim, as Terry darted forward.

"Got 'em," the boy shouted. "Let's go!"

A roar burst from the man as he scrambled to his feet, slightly dazed by the force and suddenness of the encounter. At the same time the side door of the house opened and the butler appeared. But by this time the three cadets were running like frightened deer over the lawn in the direction of the street.

"There they go!" shouted the caretaker. "Stop them!"

He began to run in their direction, but he was no match for the fleet cadets. By the time he reached the street the cadets were turning the corner a block away and were soon lost to sight. Back at the house Arthur Gates snorted with rage.

"Wait until I get dressed, Arthur," commanded the senior Gates. "Order the car out at once."

"Where are you going?" the son asked.

"Right up to the school to make the colonel pay dearly for this outrage!" shouted Melvin Gates, entering the house.

Meanwhile the three were on their way to the school, talking over their lucky escape.

"Let's take the back streets, fellows," Don advised. "There was quite an uproar at Gates' house and we don't want to meet up with any police who might be suspicious. Of course we could explain things to the chief but the thing we want to do is to get back to the school as fast as we can."

"OK," agreed Terry. "I guess we had better get into our overcoats, Jim. We're pretty heated up and we don't want to catch cold."

"No, we don't," said Jim. "Here, you hold the cup, Don."

When they had put on their coats Terry chuckled. "I want to compliment you on being a huge success as a sky rocket, Don! The way you shot down out of that tree onto that fellow's shoulders was a treat!"

"I couldn't have done it if you and Jim hadn't been so prompt to warn me of what was going on down there," said Don. "I had no idea, from up in the tree, that there was anyone else down there with you."

"He must have been prowling around and heard us up there," Jim said. "I didn't hear him come up and the first thing I knew about him was when he grabbed my shoulder. It was a good thing that he thought there were only two of us."

"When I dropped out of the tree I saw him, but it was too

122

late to do anything about it," explained Terry. "My first impulse was to yell to Don, but that would have been the worst thing I could have done."

"Yes," smiled Don. "As it was, it turned out for the best. He certainly went flying. Somebody coming fellows, and it looks like a policeman!"

"Had we better duck him?" whispered Jim.

"I think we had," admitted Don. "He must know that cadets aren't usually on the streets at this hour and the least he'll do is to question us. He may even want to go up to the school with us, and we don't want that."

"No, we don't," Terry supplied. "He hasn't seen us yet, so let's slide in here."

There was a garage close by with a narrow alley running alongside it and the boys quickly glided into it. But this particular policeman strolled right by the place and was soon lost in the darkness of the long street. When they were sure that he was safely out of sight they emerged from their hiding places.

"Whew, that was close, too," commented Terry, as they resumed their way.

"It would have been bad for us if we had been caught," admitted Jim. "Let's hustle up to the school."

The streets were all deserted and the houses black, for the hour was late. The three cadets met no one else as they hastened on to the school. They entered the grounds with a sense of profound relief.

"I hope that the colonel is still up," Don said.

"He will be," predicted Terry. "He knew what an errand we went on and he'll be waiting for us."

Terry proved to be a true prophet. When they entered the school office they found the colonel there waiting for them. He was impatiently tapping a long letter-opener on the desk, and at the sound of their entrance he sprang to his feet, glancing sharply at the clock.

"We beg to report ourselves back, Colonel Morrell," said Don, saluting and smiling at the same time. The others saluted at once and the colonel somewhat hastily returned it.

"And I'm more than glad to see you back here," the colonel exploded. "I've been worrying about you. Did you have any luck?"

"Unless I am greatly mistaken we have the cup right with us, in this box," said Don quietly. He placed it on the desk.

"We'll open it and see," the colonel stated.

A hammer was procured from a nearby closet and with a few swift blows the colonel broke open the wooden box. As the last board fell away a somewhat tarnished silver cup was disclosed to view. The colonel raised it from the box and they looked at the inscription on the side. It read: "Presented to Woodcrest Military Institute by Melvin R. Gates for Excellence in Scholastic Effort. Won by Arthur F. Gates of the Senior Class, April 7, 1933."

"That's the cup," murmured Jim.

Without a word the colonel turned it up so they could all see what was written on the bottom. All of them craned forward to read the brief message which had been written deep into the silver by the aid of a pin or knife.

The message was simple but tragic. It read: "I cheated. Arthur Gates."

There was a moment of silence on the part of the colonel and his loyal cadets. Then the colonel said very quietly, "You see what it means, boys?"

"I think I do," nodded Don in a low voice. "After Gates had promised Long that he would confess his dishonorable action he said he would write it where it would stand for good. Long didn't know what he meant by that, but when he had left the room Gates scratched that confession on the bottom of the cup with a sharp instrument."

"Yes," went on the colonel. "Long never knew of that, and during the night Gates must have experienced a change of heart, so he took the cup on the following morning. He knew that Long would expose him if he went back on his promise to confess, so he stole that cup in order to create an atmosphere that would make Long the butt of ridicule if he ever came out with the story of Gates' dishonesty."

"How can a man with any sense of common decency do a thing like that?" wondered Jim.

The colonel shrugged his shoulders. "I'm very much afraid that Arthur Gates was never a shining light of virtue. We have found out that he was dismissed from at least one school for an offense such as he committed here. You can see that he would never have the courage to face the school and say, 'Gentlemen, I cheated.' Under Long's persuasion he relented long enough to write the confession on the cup, but I guess he bitterly regretted his act later."

"The cup was a nightmare to him," said Jim. "He didn't have the nerve to take it to a jeweler, so he kept it hidden in his own house."

"Things are getting pretty bad," murmured Terry, staring at the simple confession on the cup. "A fellow can't tell a lie without having it come back after him years later!"

"That's something a man can never escape," replied the colonel briefly. "But tell me how you got the cup."

Don related his share and the other two boys had just finished telling their part in the adventure when there was the sound of a car stopping outside the school door. The sound of determined footsteps followed and then the hall door was opened. Don, guessing what was in the wind, pushed the cup from sight under the colonel's desk. A slight nod from the portly headmaster showed that he grasped the situation.

Melvin Gates strode into the office with his son Arthur at his heels. The elder Gates was fairly bristling and his son wore a blustering air that deceived no one. Melvin Gates shot a triumphant glance at the assembled party and then addressed the colonel.

"Look here, Morrell, do you know that these boys have been breaking into my house tonight?" he rasped.

"Yes," said the colonel.

"You do, eh?" shouted the irate man. "Maybe you sent them to do it, eh?"

"No," the colonel denied. "I only told them to go to your garden, but as long as they found it necessary to go into your house I'm glad of it!"

The elder Gates became purple in the face and Arthur stepped forward. "Look here, Colonel Morrell, this is no joking matter. I'm going to have these boys locked up!"

The colonel only smiled. Melvin Gates rapped the desk with his cane.

"So you teach your boys housebreaking, do you, colonel?" he cried.

"Why no," said the colonel, thoughtfully. "That isn't part of the program. But we do teach them to play the game of life honorably and to put forth every ounce of their strength to find out the truth and do the square thing!"

"Oh, what nonsense are you talking now?" growled Melvin Gates.

The eyes of the colonel blazed as he reached under his

desk and brought up the silver cup. "This is the preaching that speaks for itself, Gates. After you have taken a good look at the bottom of this cup I want to hear you say that you intend to lock my boys up!"

The faces of the two turned pale when they saw the inscription on the bottom of the cup. Melvin shot an angry glance at his son.

"I told you to get rid of that thing long ago," he cried.

"These boys have been after that cup for months, Mr. Gates," went on the colonel. "It was for that purpose that they broke into your house tonight, and I want you to understand definitely that I heartily back them up, and so will the world in general when it knows the story."

"But see here, Morrell, you are surely not going to let this thing get out?" begged Melvin Gates. "I have shielded this boy of mine from his folly and weakness for years, and it will be perfectly terrible if it gets out now. Think of our good name in this town, man!"

"How many times have you and your son thought of George Long, carrying the stigma of a thief all of these years?" blazed the colonel, seeming to swell up in his honest wrath. "Have you ever given him or his name any consideration? If it was simply a case of covering up a weak moral escapade of your boy which had not hurt anyone but himself I would gladly help you by saying nothing. But you have had no thought for the burden that George Long has been compelled to carry with him. Under the circumstances I have no sympathy for you, Mr. Gates, and I warn you that Long shall be cleared publicly as soon as possible."

"Colonel Morrell," said Melvin Gates, putting on an air of cunning that turned the boys against him even more, "I have a little money in this world. Now, if we can come to some sort of an agreement on this thing, I'll make it well worth—"

But the colonel became red in the face with suppressed anger. He pointed toward the door.

"Get out of my school, both of you!" he quivered. "I won't have my clean young boys insulted by your presence here any longer. If you think you can buy my tongue with your money you are badly mistaken, Melvin Gates. Please take your son and leave the school at once, sir."

Realizing that any more talk would be a pure waste of time the father and son withdrew, gloom written on their faces.

When they had gone the colonel turned to his grave-faced cadets.

"Boys, your work is over, and you may report to your quarters. If any discipline officer says anything to you because of absence from your rooms tonight, refer him to me. I commend you on your interest and courage in this matter, and Mr. Long shall know the full particulars. The cadet corps will be proud of you. Goodnight, boys."

Silently the cadets saluted, returned the colonel's goodnight and went to their room.

Chapter 24
The Alumni Dance

"I see the next Alumni affair will be a dance," Don remarked, looking across the table to Jim, who was studying.

"Yes. Looking in the *Bombardment*, are you?" his brother replied.

"Sure. I guess that is the affair at which Colonel Morrell intends to clear George Long," Don went on.

"It is. There will be a dinner and a dance and then the colonel will tell his story. It will be a pleasant evening for Long and his wife."

"Goodness knows they have it coming to them," mused Don. "I'd hate to go around for a number of years with a cloud like that hanging over me. If I met an old fellow student I'd have to be prepared to see suspicion showing in his face or even to meet with outspoken slighting. It has been a fearful burden and I'm glad that it is to be lifted soon."

"So am I," agreed Jim. "Mr. Long must think we have forgotten him, though. So many months have gone by since we went to see him about the matter. Here it is the last of February already."

"Yes, time has passed rapidly. It won't be long before the spring is at hand."

"That was a terrible tongue-lashing that the colonel gave Gates the other night, wasn't it?"

"Nothing more than he deserved," retorted Don, promptly. "Just imagine, he wanted to pay the colonel to keep quiet and let Long go on with this blight on his good name! Just as the colonel said, if the whole thing had been some failing of the son's in which he had injured no one but himself, why we'd all be glad to keep still and give the man a chance. But that particular type of outrage calls for extreme measures."

"Right you are. Where is that red-headed friend of ours?"

"Out visiting," grinned Don. "That boy surely has a multitude of friends!"

Terry returned to the room just before the lights went out and brought some news with him. But before he told them the news he played one of the tricks of which he was so very fond. When he approached the room he tapped on the door sharply, turned the knob and stepped briskly into the room. Imitating to perfection the tones of Officer of the Section he called out:

"Attention, gentlemen! Stand at attention for inspection, please!"

Once a day their rooms were rigidly inspected and although the officer of that section was not in the habit of calling them to attention so pointedly the boys fell into the trap. Terry's voice was so like that of the officer that the two boys put down their books, leaped to their feet and were just about ready to stand at attention when they caught sight of the grinning face of their friend.

"Ho, ha!" roared Terry, seeing the look of disgust on their faces. "Wasn't that a pretty picture? I almost expected you to salute, gentlemen!"

"We're going to salute you so that you won't sit down for some time to come," growled Jim, moving around the table with his chemistry book in his hands. Don leaped at Terry and bore him to the bed. The red-head was too weak to offer any resistance and Jim paddled him vigorously with the book, until he cried for mercy.

"I just heard something that will interest you," Terry said, when the fooling had stopped.

"What is it?" asked Jim. "Out with it, or we'll paddle you some more!"

"The Gates family has moved out of town!" Terry said.

"I'm glad of it," cried Don, promptly. "I've always thought it too bad that such rascals should live in that fine, historic old place."

"That isn't such a sanctified place," observed Jim. "Don't forget the spy that lived there."

"But the spy had even purer motives in life than the Gates family did," Don defended. "The house is really a historic relic and I think some fine American family ought to live in it."

"I see your point," nodded Jim. "So the Gates' skipped, did they?"

"Yes, moved out completely," Terry replied. "No one seems to know just where they did go. Of course, they were dreading the time when the colonel will tell the truth about them."

"Oh, sure," Don said. "Well, we're not a bit sorry to see the last of them. For a number of years the school has actually suffered from contact with father and son and nothing is lost by their going."

"By the way," observed Terry. "What is to be done about the matter of that scholarship that Woodcrest won so many years ago from Roxberry? When the story is published the preparatory school will find out that we didn't win the contest fairly."

"I imagine that it will be held all over again, or the matter entirely dropped," Jim said. "I'm pretty sure that Roxberry won't care to say much when they find that one of their professors gave Gates the list of questions before the exams."

That proved to be the case. The scholarship contest was never held again and nothing was said by the Roxberry Alumni when the story got into the papers. As for the dishonest professor, nothing more was ever heard of him.

Just before the Alumni Dance certain cadets were appointed for the posts of honor at the affair. A good many of the first classmen served as waiters, but the cadets who had been most active in the establishing of George Long's innocence were given posts of honor at the long tables at which the guests ate. In this class Don, Jim, Terry, Hudson, Douglas and Vench found themselves on the night of the affair.

The colonel had made it a point to gather together all of the men of the former 1933 class who could come and he was delighted to find that all but five members of that class were present. Three of these men lay in graves overseas and many more from that class were ex-servicemen from the United States Army. Two members lived so far away that they were unable to get there. Many from other classes were there and it was an impressive gathering.

Mr. and Mrs. Long entered late and were just in time to sit down at the table. The cadets and the colonel felt that Long had been purposely late, so as not to have to face any unpleasantness that would have spoiled Mrs. Long's evening. Long had in his heart another and more chivalrous purpose, of which his wife alone was aware. He did not want to make any of his former classmates feel cheap by cutting him at first and then having to apologize afterward.

The cadets were seated at the head of each table, a procedure that puzzled the members of the alumni, for they had never seen such an arrangement before, and they wondered why it had been done. They were not long in finding out. After the dishes had been cleared away the colonel arose. Beside him, on either side, sat Mr. and Mrs. Long, purposely placed there so that no one could slight them. The colonel spoke amidst an impressive silence.

"Gentlemen of the Alumni Association, I wish to tell you a story that combines all the elements of tragedy, drama and fine courage. I will waste no words in telling it for I predict that after I am through you will all of you have some hand-shaking and talking to do. I wish the members of the class of 1933 to pay special attention to my story."

Here the colonel reached under the table and brought forth the class cup which had been the cause of all the trouble and placed it on the table. A murmur went around and Long turned pale with conflicting emotions. And in the silence that followed the colonel carefully and quietly told the whole story.

"And gentlemen," wound up the colonel, when the murmurs of amazement and indignation had subsided, "I wish to present to you the cadets you have just heard about. These are the men who tracked this thing to its lair. Mr. Donald Mercer, Mr. James Mercer, Mr. Hudson, Mr. Vench, Mr. Douglas and Mr. Mackson, please stand up so that everyone can see who you are."

A storm of handclapping greeted the modest cadets as they stood in their places and instinctively the men of the school alumni stood up and saluted the red-faced cadets. With a sense of the fitness of things the uniformed cadets briskly returned the salutes and sat down. The colonel now turned to Mr. Long.

"Mr. Long, please stand up." As Long obeyed: "Gentlemen of the Alumni, there is nothing that is necessary for me to say, except that in the name of the school I apologize for the tremendous wrong done Mr. Long. I present to you gentlemen in all his unspotted honor Cadet Captain George Long!"

This time the present cadets rose with the company and clapped heartily for George Long. Tears ran down Mrs. Long's face and she was not in the least ashamed for them. When the applause had died down Long said a few words to the assembled men, thanking such of them who had believed in him and graciously excusing those to whom the facts had looked so black that they could not help suspecting him. Then the supper formation broke up and Long was deluged with those who wished to shake his hand and express their delight and beg his pardon for their past conduct.

The cadets came in for an overwhelming amount of praise and then the entire body of alumni and their wives went over to the school hall for dancing. Both Mr. and Mrs. Long embarrassed the boys with their thanks and praise. During the evening all of the honor cadets danced with Mrs. Long.

When it was all over the boys went back to their room and prepared for bed. The evening had been a happy one for them and they discussed it gravely, thankful for their opportunity to have been of service to George Long.

"It must have been a wonderful feeling for him," Don remarked, as he washed for bed.

"Yes, indeed," agreed Terry. "It was a happy evening for Mrs. Long, too."

"I'd rather be George Long, with all his years of carrying the shadow, than Arthur Gates, whose life has practically been a failure," Jim observed.

"You're dead right," Don assented. "Well, now the mystery is solved, and I wonder what we'll do next? Settle down to a tame life, probably."

On the following morning they looked out of the windows at a bleak, rain-washed day. Jim growled in disgust.

"Golly, what rain!" he grumbled. "It is fairly coming down in buckets. That means indoor sports for a time."

"Yes, and it looks like the kind of a rain that lasts a while," sighed Don.

Terry grinned with his usual cheerfulness. "Don't let a little water dampen your spirits, my boys," he advised. "A little rain won't alter our lives!"

www.ingramcontent.com/pod-product-compliance
Lightning Source LLC
Chambersburg PA
CBHW011448170626
46816CB00008B/2576